SEARCH FOR THE STAR

Read all the Unicorns of Balinor books:

UNICORNS OF BALINOR

SEARCH FOR THE STAR

MARY STANTON

AN
APPLE
PAPERBACK

SCHOLASTIC INC.
New York Toronto London Auckland Sydney
Mexico City New Delhi Hong Kong

Cover illustration by D. Craig

No part of this publication may be reproduced, stored in a retrieval system, or transmitted in any form or by any means, electronic, mechanical, photocopying, recording, or otherwise, without written permission of the publisher. For information regarding permission, write to Scholastic Inc., Attention: Permissions Department, 555 Broadway, New York, NY 10012.

ISBN 0-439-12047-0

Text copyright © 1999 by Mary Stanton
Cover illustration © 1999 by Scholastic Inc.
All rights reserved. Published by Scholastic Inc.
SCHOLASTIC, APPLE PAPERBACKS, and associated logos are trademarks and/or registered trademarks of Scholastic Inc.
UNICORNS OF BALINOR is a trademark of Scholastic Inc.

12 11 10 9 8 7 6 5 4 3   0 1 2 3 4/0

Printed in the U.S.A.
First Scholastic printing, November 1999

For Julie and Jason Schwartz,
who already know the secret

SEARCH FOR THE STAR

1

Atalanta stood at the Watching Pool and greeted the first faint whisper of dawn with a whicker of happiness. All was peaceful in the Celestial Valley. The ceremony to greet the sun would take place soon. Every morning, the unicorns of the Celestial Valley assembled to form the rainbow under the Crystal Arch. The rainbow herd sang to the sun as it rose over the Eastern Ridge. Each unicorn was a separate color, and the vivid crimsons, scarlets, emeralds, yellows, and blues made a splendid sight.

Atalanta dipped her crystal horn in the waters of the Watching Pool in a brief farewell. Now she was ready to take her place at the head of the twilight band — the blue, indigo, violet end of the rainbow — as was her right. She shook herself, her creamy mane flowing around her withers, and pivoted on her hind legs, ready to race across the green field to the arch.

A low and evil laugh rose from the Watching Pool.

Atalanta turned back. The water in the Watching Pool was bubbling! A vision appeared in the center.

Atalanta shivered. This was wrong. She was the Dreamspeaker! She alone summoned the visions from the Watching Pool. What terrible magic was at work, that the images would come unbidden?

She leaned over the waters, her breath a light mist in the predawn air.

And she saw . . .

A monstrous mountain rising high over the land of Balinor. Its peak stretched almost beyond the sky. Its stony sides were sheathed in ice. In the daytime, when the sun was high, the crags and hollows of this giant mound reflected the sky's own blue.

This was Blue Mountain. It was very old: Its shadow had been cast over Balinor since time itself began. There were legends among the unicorns of the Celestial Valley about the mountain. Some said it was the first home of the Old Mare of the Mountain; others said that the Deep Magic itself began in the caves beneath the mountain's feet.

Atalanta herself, Dreamspeaker to the Celestial herd — and the wisest of that immortal breed of unicorns — didn't know for certain. But all knew who lived there: Naytin the giant dragon, guardian of the Indigo Star.

Atalanta leaned closer over the banks of the Watching Pool. The Indigo Star was the greatest source of magic in Balinor and all the worlds beyond. Naytin the dragon was a fierce and terrible protector of the Star's magic.

Who would send Atalanta a vision of Blue Mountain? And why?

She drew back from the Watching Pool, worry clouding her violet eyes.

All knew who lived in the shadow of Blue Mountain. The mountain towered over Demonview and the Valley of Fear. There, in the middle of the Fiery Field, not far from the Pit where slaves labored day after weary day, lay Castle Entia. Home of Entia, the Shifter: usurper of the throne of Balinor, sworn enemy of the Celestial Valley herd.

The Dreamspeaker thought intently for a long moment. Then she dipped her crystal horn in the waters three times. "I call on the Shifter," she said steadily. Her voice was low and sweet, with no hint of fear.

The image of Blue Mountain faded away. A new image came instead. Atalanta saw a valley, hideous with pits of fire. On the horizon was a castle, dark and ominous.

The Valley of Fear — and Castle Entia.

A huge, winged beast rose from the courtyard of Castle Entia and beat its slow, strong way to Blue Mountain. Black, roiling smoke obscured the flyer. As the cloud rose toward the mountain's highest reaches, winds blew the smoke aside. Atalanta jumped back, quivering.

It was Entia, the Shifter! Feared by all for his ability to transform himself into any shape he desired. He was now a giant unicorn, black as coal and twice the height of his enemy the bronze stallion known as the Sunchaser. His horn was a deadly spike of iron. Wings twice as long as his muscular body sprang from his shoulders and beat the air with strong, rhythmic strokes.

Atalanta stared at the vision in the Watching Pool with horror in her heart.

The Shifter flew straight to Blue Mountain. Straight to the Indigo Star.

2

Entia's lips drew back with the effort of his climb into the sky. His teeth were fanged, and his eyes were pits of fire. His nostrils flared crimson with the effort of breathing in the thinning air. His iron hooves glowed red-hot. He could feel the strength in his wings, the rush of cold air through the oily feathers.

He rejoiced in the evil magic that had given him his wings. Wings that would get him to Blue Mountain just in time. He was enraptured by flight. There was power in it, more power than any other unicorn would ever know. And it was this power of flight that would help him conquer Balinor for all time.

A burst of angry flame came from his muzzle as he flew — as he remembered.

He had won — he had been supreme — until he'd lost the Royal Scepter. Until that meddling fool, the Sunchaser, and his lady-mistress, Princess Arianna, had stolen the Scepter back.

Entia was supreme no longer! The anger he felt in his heart made the muscles of his broad chest quiver as he circled the mountain.

All was *not* lost. Not yet. There was another source of power that could challenge the magic of the Royal Scepter. That power was known as the Indigo Star — a huge, shining, midnight-blue jewel hidden deep inside Blue Mountain, in Naytin's lair, under the dragon's belly. Lost in the mists of legends, even the cursed Dreamspeaker did not know when Naytin, guardian of the Indigo Star, would wake to terrorize the skies again.

But Entia knew. Naytin woke from its magic sleep once every thousand years. It was a slow waking. The dragon, motionless for a millennium, would twist and thrash as it began to arise. The waking would take days. But in the first hour, as the dragon's consciousness swam up from the deep ocean of sleep, Naytin would move.

The Indigo Star lay under the tip of Naytin's gigantic scaly tail. And when it moved, Entia would have one chance to snatch it. One chance to dart and weave and take the Star from beneath the shelter of that mighty tail.

It would be no simple task to retrieve the jewel, but these were desperate times and the

Shifter was not ready to give up his dreams of conquest.

There — the Shifter saw a crevice in the face of the mountain and a ledge near it upon which to land. The evil unicorn beat his massive wings and settled down on the rocks with a clack and clatter of hooves. He was so high up on Blue Mountain that he stood in the clouds. When he gazed down at the forest below, the trees looked as small as blades of grass. The air was cold; the Shifter didn't like the cold. He had come to relish the harsh and bitter heat of Castle Entia, the flaming pits of the Fiery Field.

He returned his attention to the crevice. As a unicorn, he was far too large to fit through it, but he felt a wisp of warm air on his nose. The crevice ran deep, maybe as deep as the dragon's lair.

How best to follow the trail of warm air? If the Shifter's guess was right, the warmth he felt on his nose came from the heat rising off of the dragon's sleeping body. And where Naytin lay, so lay the Indigo Star.

He would shift. He would call on the shadow magic that made him what he was. The shifting magic was his — and his alone. No other creature in Balinor could change shape at will.

The Shifter lowered his head to his chest and closed his bloodred eyes. His fangs glittered in the thin sun. Slowly, slowly, he shifted into a pillar of smoke. He curled and twisted around the rocks and entered the crevice. He strained at the effort. This worried the Shifter. Already he was beginning to feel the loss of the Royal Scepter. Until he retrieved it, or until he held the Indigo Star, his magic would weaken and weaken and soon he would be no more powerful than any of his enemies. He must act now, while he still had the remains of his power to aid him.

Down and down the Shifter went. Sometimes the crevice opened into wide subterranean passages with icy stalks of stalactites hanging from the walls. Sometimes the crevice narrowed to the width of a wormhole. He would not be able to leave the mountain the same way he'd entered it, not with the Indigo Star in tow. It was rumored that the jewel was as large as the fist of a giant. The Shifter would need the Star's magic to find his way out.

The air grew warmer. Now it also carried an animal smell — some foul combination of sweat and meat and ancient filth. The Shifter was getting closer.

Suddenly, the crevice opened up into a deep cavern.

On the floor slept Naytin, the legendary dragon of Blue Mountain.

The beast was *huge* — larger than the main hall of the Shifter's own castle. Its head was the size of an entire unicorn, and its teeth protruded like long, sharp swords. Naytin's hide was rutted and marbled and thick with moldy growth, but underneath the filth was a grand and ancient silvery hue that lit up the entire cavern.

Since the Shifter had gained his evil powers he had not known fear. Not until now. Even he could never have imagined a beast so monstrous.

The Shifter pushed aside his fear and shifted into a unicorn again. He used his wings to settle softly, silently onto the cavern floor. He had heard a tale that the dragon rested over a vast treasure — a fortune of silver and gold and priceless jewels. But he saw no such treasure beneath the dragon's hide. The Shifter was neither surprised nor disappointed to discover that this legend of gold and jewels was not true. His muzzle parted in a grim smile. Many humans had lost their lives on the mountain in pursuit of nothing. Humans were greedy in a way that unicorns were not. The Shifter cared little for golden trinkets or precious metals. It was the Indigo Star he wanted — for its magic — for its power.

He took one step forward, then two.

If the great dragon sensed his presence and awakened sooner than the legend said — well, the Shifter refused to think about that. Without the Royal Scepter, he would be no match for the dragon. He would be crushed to death by one swipe of Naytin's massive tail. Or perhaps the dragon would turn its powerful breath against him — a breath that was rumored to blow hurricanes across the land.

Naytin groaned. The thousand-year sleep was over. The awakening was beginning.

The dragon groaned again. Its tail jerked as it began the long climb up from sleep. Entia stepped back and stiffened. His lips drew back in a terrible grin of pleasure. There, beneath the dragon's tail! A midnight jewel in the shape of a six-pointed star glimmered with a magical light.

The Shifter's excitement now replaced his fear. He used his shifting magic to alter his foreleg into a monstrous arm and hand. The hand was twice as large as a human's, with nine long fingers and a thumb shaped like a giant hook.

The Shifter reached forward.

The dragon stirred.

The Shifter growled softly. But Naytin did not wake.

The Shifter reached forward again, and this time he closed his newly formed hand around the Indigo Star. He carefully worked it back and forth, inch by inch.

Finally, the Shifter freed the Indigo Star from beneath the dragon's tail. He held the jewel in his hand.

What power! The Star's blue radiance flooded the cave! Entia curled his talons around the jewel. His body throbbed with the pulse of magic.

He had held the Royal Scepter, too, but the Star was stronger.

With the magic of the Indigo Star at his command, no one could defeat him!

Naytin, the great dragon, stirred again. This time there was no fear in the Shifter's heart. He stared at the dragon in speculation, his eyes narrowed, his breath an evil stream of smoke in the cavern's air. Was there a way to use the dragon to help him defeat his enemies? He could turn Naytin against the humans, send the beast out with its hurricane breath to destroy Balinor. All of Balinor would know that the Shifter had captured the Indigo Star, and that the dragon served him — the Shifter!

All would bow at his feet then. Even the high and mighty Princess Arianna and her cherished unicorn! All would fear him!

And as for Atalanta?

The Shifter twisted the Star and let its pale blue light wash over his arm. He held it up, bathed in the wash of magic.

As for Atalanta . . . He could wait for his revenge on the Princess and her Bonded unicorn. But he could not — would not — wait to wreak havoc on the Dreamspeaker.

He chuckled softly. Ah, yes. He knew to what use he would put the Indigo Star first. The Dreamspeaker and her beloved Celestial unicorns would feel the force of his magic. She was the lead mare of the twilight band of their precious rainbow herd. And that coat of hers — deep violet. A color he'd always despised.

Laughter bubbled from his throat. The sound spilled into the cave like a polluted stream.

"Atalanta! — SEE WHAT I HAVE FOR YOU!"

3

Atalanta raced across the emerald-green grasslands of the Celestial Valley. Her violet coat was damp with sweat. Her silver mane whipped around her crystal horn. She halted briefly at the banks of the Imperial River. No time to gallop around the bend beyond. No time!

She leaped into the river. She swam with all her might against the strong current. Her delicate forelegs churned. River water sprayed her nose and eyes and ears. Once ashore, she galloped toward the Eastern Ridge, to the Crystal Arch.

Fear and desperation clutched at her heart. She ran because she *must* talk to the Old Mare of the Mountain. The Old Mare had to have an answer! She ran because —

And then Atalanta realized that she was not running alone. The other unicorns of the Celestial Valley galloped with her, not far behind, just now crossing the river. She had spooked them. She hadn't intended that. But she was frightened, terribly frightened, and she had panicked without thinking.

She stopped and forced herself to be calm. This would never do. She was Dreamspeaker to the Celestial Valley herd, mate to Numinor, the Golden One. No matter what happened to her and to her kind, she must face the outer world with dignity. She walked toward the Crystal Arch with her head high, her breathing slow and deliberate.

Atalanta saw a few Celestial unicorns gathering for the rainbow ceremony. But not the blue band! The twilight band's colors were fading! And with the fading of their color would come the loss of their magic! The indigos, sapphires, and her own violet would disappear forever!

Tears sparkled in her lavender eyes but she blinked them back fiercely. She took her position at the base of the Crystal Arch. The huge oak gateway towered over her. Through those doors, the Celestial unicorns could travel down to the world below, into Balinor, where the humans lived. But another stairway led up to the sky heavens, where the Old Mare reigned next to the One Who Rules.

Behind her, the Celestial Valley herd assembled silently. On the flanks of the Eastern Ridge, Numinor himself came down like a bright golden cloud. Atalanta lifted her head and whinnied at him. He was so beautiful! His coat was as golden as the sun. The precious golden diamond that held his personal magic glittered.

But for how long? Atalanta asked herself. *For how long?* For if the blue band lost its color — would the other colors of the rainbow herd be far behind?

She waited until Numinor stepped to her side. They exchanged a long, long look. Then Atalanta stepped forward and knocked her horn on the door to the sky, the door that led to the land of the One Who Rules. The three knocks echoed loudly across the mountain range.

"Old One!" Atalanta called. Her voice was sweet, as it had always been. But it trembled a little. The unicorns behind her stirred uneasily. "I must talk to you immediately!"

No answer. The doors remained sealed behind their giant iron clasps. Atalanta heard the other unicorns coming up swiftly behind her.

"*Please*, Old One," Atalanta said.

The Celestial unicorns came to a halt behind her. Atalanta could feel their concern. They were frightened, too.

A boulder at the base of the ridge began to take the shape of a unicorn — first its head, then its neck, body, and legs. At last, the boulder transformed into the Old Mare. Her shaggy coat and aged eyes looked more tired than Atalanta had remembered them.

"Old One," Atalanta said, and bowed her

head gracefully to the ground. The unicorns behind her did the same.

The Old Mare of the Mountain nodded gravely back. "So," she said grimly. "The colors of the blue band are beginning to fade."

Atalanta nodded. "It just began as the sun started to rise. My own color . . ." She raised her right foreleg. The lavender-twilight color of her pasterns had turned a ghostly white. "And of course, the colors of those in the blue band are fading first because the blue band is the beginning of the rainbow! Does this mean that the other bands will fade, too?"

The Old Mare didn't answer. But there was sorrow in her eyes.

"In the Watching Pool, early this morning, a vision came of its own accord," Atalanta said. "I did not summon it. It was of Blue Mountain, where Naytin sleeps. I wondered why I should see this place, and why the image should come unbidden.

"I called on the Watching Pool to show me the Shifter. Although I could not — would not — believe that even he would dare to confront the guardian of the Indigo Star, I saw Entia leave his castle and fly toward Blue Mountain! If he has something to do with this draining away of our colors . . ." She suddenly could not speak. Tears threatened to steal her resolve.

"Approach me," the Old Mare said, her voice

neither commanding nor threatening, but heavy with sadness.

Atalanta stepped forward. She had never been so close to the Old Mare. For the first time, Atalanta could see how fragile she was. Her horn was almost translucent with age. "If the unicorns lose their color — what has happened, Old One? What evil magic is the Shifter using that can steal the colors of the Celestial unicorns right off our backs?"

The Old Mare's eyes closed in a spasm of grief. Then she looked at Atalanta. "Only an ancient magic — a magic even older than I. I felt it immediately. It could only be the Indigo Star. The balance of power in our world has shifted again. The forces of evil will soon strike fear into the hearts of everyone."

Atalanta's legs suddenly felt weak. "How could this have happened? When Princess Arianna captured the Royal Scepter and won the trial by fire and the ordeal by moonlight, I thought that things would be better, that we had finally gained the advantage. I had hoped that the Shifter would soon be defeated."

"We all hoped the same thing," the Old Mare said. "But now the Shifter has stolen the Indigo Star."

Atalanta's heart froze. The Star's magic was like the force of water over a mighty falls. No one knew the source of the magic — but the magic could be directed by the one who possessed the

Star. And if the Shifter had it, it would be the end of them all.

Atalanta closed her eyes and despaired. The color of her coat was magical; it flowed from the jewel at the base of her horn. If she lost her color . . . without her personal magic, she could no longer protect Princess Arianna and the Sunchaser from the Shifter. She could no longer send dreams, nor walk the path below to Balinor.

The Old Mare's sharp voice jerked her eyes open. Her old eyes looked directly at the Dreamspeaker. "From this point forward, you must be a pillar of strength for the others. They will look to you for guidance and wisdom. If you are afraid, they will also be afraid. If you lose hope, they will lose hope. Things will get worse before they get better, and you must not allow the Celestial unicorns to lose heart."

"Will the Star's magic obey the Shifter's will?" asked Atalanta hopelessly. "Can it be bent to do evil as well as good?"

"You know the answer to that, Atalanta. The Deep Magic can be bent and twisted. It has no sense of good or evil. It is power. Like fire. Like a mighty windstorm."

"A terrible power," Atalanta said sadly.

The Old Mare nodded. "More powerful than anyone could have imagined. The Indigo Star has been safely nestled under the great dragon Naytin for centuries. Until now."

"How can there be magic so strong that it can steal the colors of the unicorns?" she asked desperately. But Atalanta feared she knew the answer to this.

The Old Mare shook her head. "The Shifter hates the colors of the rainbow herd. And what he hates, he will try to destroy."

"We will stop him," Atalanta said. Her pride was beginning to return, along with her strength of resolve. Behind her, the Celestial herd murmured assent.

"There is only one power that can defeat the Shifter now. You must combine the Royal Scepter with the Indigo Star. There is no magic stronger in all the world than the Scepter and the Star together."

"How can we steal the Star from the Shifter?"

But the Old Mare began to disappear, turning back into rock. Her voice was a mere thread. Atalanta had to bend forward to hear. "You and the Princess Arianna must find a way. This will determine the fate of our entire world. If evil prevails, all of the colors will fade. The Shifter will rule the land and all who dwell there will be shadows in his power. Animals, humans, and unicorns alike. There will come a terrible Age of Darkness."

"How can I tell them?" Atalanta said, fearing to glance behind her at the Celestial unicorns. "It will break their hearts."

"A fight will soon fall upon them, and they must be prepared. Do you understand?"

Atalanta nodded. "Thank you, Old One, for your honesty."

"That's one thing you'll always get from me," said the Old Mare. Then she sighed deeply. The transformation back to rock was complete.

Atalanta was alone at the foot of the Crystal Arch. She bowed her head, collecting herself. Then she turned to face the Celestial unicorns. She felt a mountain breeze caress her flanks. The air carried the scent of pine and cedar. If there was evil afoot, no one would know it — not here in the Celestial Valley, where peace, beauty, and harmony had reigned forever.

The Celestial unicorns looked expectantly at her. She would stand tall and proud and tell them everything, just as the Old Mare had advised. She would not cry anymore. Tears were useless. These were the strongest, bravest unicorns in all the land, and soon they would have to prove their will. She would lead them as best she could.

And, of course, she would not be alone.

There was Sunchaser and Rednal and Tobiano. They were gone from the Celestial Valley right now, heading back to Balinor in the company of the Princess Arianna. There was her loyal mate, Numinor, even now looking at her proudly. There was the Princess Arianna herself, returned to Balinor with the Royal Scepter in hand. And there were the humans of Balinor, strong and clever and courageous in their own right, who were willing to fight against the forces of evil. There would be no Age of Darkness, Atalanta promised herself, as long as she had breath to fight.

As long as they all fought together.

4

Captain Tredwell's sailors brought the *Dawnwalker* smoothly into the port of Sixton. Princess Arianna watched from the deck, her bronze unicorn, Sunchaser, at her side. The ship's huge sails dropped, and men threw lines ashore for the ground crew to secure the *Dawnwalker* to its dock. The crew onboard waved and shouted greetings to those on land. "Hi-ho! Hi-ho!"

The port of Sixton was busily awake. Balinor unicorns drew carts loaded with food and goods through the cobbled streets. Men and women dressed in colorful hues bustled through the seaside market. They glanced up at the beautiful ship and smiled at the sight of Sunchaser standing proudly in the stern. His ebony horn glinted in the early sun. His bronze mane rippled in the gentle sea breeze.

Princess Arianna turned to face her friends.

The Royal Scepter hung in the folds of her long red skirt, tied to her belt with a triple knot. The battle to get it back had been fierce. And she couldn't have succeeded without her loyal friends. She smiled at them: Finn, the red-haired boy from Deridia; Lincoln, her mahogany-and-black collie; Tobiano and Rednal, unicorns from the Celestial Valley; and, finally, the girl from the other side of the Gap, Lori Carmichael.

"I wonder if the people in the village know who we are?" Princess Arianna mused aloud. She had told Finn, finally, who she really was and what her future would be. Finn and the mighty unicorn Rednal had helped her pass the trial by fire and the ordeal by moonlight. Finn hadn't known then that she was Her Royal Highness, the Princess Arianna, and that Chase was the Sunchaser, Lord of the Animals in Balinor.

Now Finn's manner toward her had changed. He seemed almost afraid of her rank.

"I hope they do not know, milady." Chase's voice was grave. He rested his muzzle briefly on her shoulder. "It is still too dangerous to reveal ourselves. We must get back to Balinor Village and discuss our position with Samlett and the other leaders of the Resistance before we can meet the Shifter out in the open."

"We will win this time," Ari said. She drew in a deep breath. "We have the Royal Scepter, Chase.

And Entia has nothing to compare with its magic. We'll find my family — and take back the throne of Balinor!"

Chase nodded. His dark eyes were fierce. "We will indeed, milady!"

"When are we getting off this tub?" Tobiano grumbled.

Ari knew the black-and-white unicorn wasn't all that fond of boats. She smoothed his forelock back from his horn. "Just a few minutes more, Toby."

"Not too soon for me, either," Lori said.

Ari turned back to the port of Sixton. It was early morning. The sun was up and the sea was as calm as a field of wheat. The night before had been much less pleasant. A storm had hit in the middle of the night, and the ship had lurched, rolled, swayed, and pitched in the darkness, at the mercy of the swelling waves. Lori had been seasick, and Ari had come close to it herself. She would have been very ill if Chase hadn't dipped his horn into a cup of water and made her drink the liquid down. She had given some to Lori and it had soothed her as well.

The crewman lowered the ship-to-shore planks, and Lori was the first person off the *Dawnwalker*, her legs still wobbly and her face ashen.

"I will never, ever, EVER go on that ship again!" she said.

"Nobody asked you to come in the first place," Toby pointed out.

This was perfectly true. Lori had followed Ari

and Chase uninvited through the Gap from Glacier River Farm. And Toby, who was famed for his blunt speaking, wasn't the sort of unicorn to let anyone get away with whining.

Ari saw that Toby was about to scold Lori again, when Finn said tactfully, "It's all right, Lori. I got seasick, too."

Lori's expression changed abruptly. Ari had never seen her anger disappear so quickly. "Well," she said, "I guess it wasn't all that bad. You were probably a lot sicker than I was."

Finn winked at Ari. "I bet I was, Lori!"

"Just stick close to me," Lori said. She smoothed her hair. "I can help you with everything. I've been through danger like you wouldn't believe, let me tell you." She bounced cheerfully down the gangplank to the dock.

Ari looked at her other traveling companions in astonishment.

"Well!" said Lincoln. The collie cocked his head, his eyes mischievous. "The trip back to Balinor Village is going to be a lot easier with Finn along!"

Ari didn't say anything. She watched Finn help Lori over a bale of wool. Lori batted her eyelashes at him, then she giggled too loudly at something Finn said. Finn's red hair curled along the back of his neck. His eyes were a clear brown in his suntanned face. Lori obviously thought he was very good-looking.

"Do you think he's good-looking?" Ari whispered to Chase.

"Beauty is in the eye of the beholder," the Royal Scepter said before Chase could reply. Which, Ari thought, was probably a good thing, since her unicorn looked totally bewildered at this impulsive question from his mistress. "There are two options," the Scepter continued in its bossy way. "One: The boy Finn is —"

"Quiet!" Ari closed her hand firmly around the carved wooden unicorn head at the top of the Scepter. The Scepter was filled with magic of a deep and powerful kind. She didn't know how to use it just yet; for that, she would have to speak to Atalanta. But she did know how to keep it quiet when it answered the wrong question.

She had hoped Atalanta would come to her in her dreams last night. Perhaps the terrible storm had prevented it, or tonight she might appear when they were on the road to Balinor Village. The Dreamspeaker would know the secrets of the Royal Scepter.

In the meantime, it was very annoying to have the Scepter answer any question she asked — whether she wanted answers or not. Ari appreciated the Scepter's help, but it was an exasperating bit of magic all the same. "Let's go, Chase," she said abruptly. "Do you think we can get to the Unicorn Inn by nightfall tomorrow?"

The Royal Scepter didn't waste any time in

26

answering *that* question: "If we maintain an average speed of . . ." Ari tucked the Royal Scepter under her leather vest. Even if Finn did keep Lori from throwing temper tantrums every three minutes, it was going to be a long, long trip home.

5

Ari's journey back to Balinor Village was peaceful. Rednal volunteered to draw the hired carriage. The first day's journey from Sixton to Balinor Village was, for the most part, calm and quiet. Everyone seemed to welcome the slow pace and uneventful day. Finn and Lori sat in the carriage and kept busy chatting with each other; Lincoln and Toby spent a lot of time running out ahead of the carriage, exploring the countryside; and Ari rode Chase and watched what was happening in her family's kingdom.

This far south of the Valley of Fear, it was hard to see evidence of the Shifter's reign. Farmers still plowed the fields, unicorns pulled people and goods in carts along the busy roads, and people went about their daily business. But the good cheer and laughter Ari remembered from the days before the Shifter took over her father's Palace wasn't abroad in her country at all.

People were less trusting. And always, always, they would watch the skies, fearful of seeing the Shifter's black, oily wings beating through the air.

Ari stopped the journey as the sun went down. Finn made camp in a little glade midway between Sixton and Balinor. Finn was a huge help. Somehow, he charmed Lori into gathering wood branches for a fire. He drew water from the stream running through the meadow, set up a small camping kitchen with supplies from the rented wagon, and created a wonderful vegetable stew for supper. Rednal, Chase, and Toby rolled luxuriously in the thick grass, then settled down to a nice long graze. Lincoln followed Ari around for a bit, then curled up by the fire and went to sleep.

Ari found herself with nothing to do. After supper, with night drawing in, the stew pot scrubbed clean, the others followed Lincoln's example and slept. Ari sat with her knees drawn up to her chin and gazed into the fire. She so wanted to speak with Atalanta!

Atalanta sent news to the humans in Balinor in two ways. The first way was in dreams as the twilight-colored unicorn spoke softly of events to come and events that had been. The other way was through emissaries such as Tobiano and Rednal.

And on rare occasions, Ari had actually seen her in person.

The Royal Scepter poked uncomfortably into her hip. Her head nodded forward, her eyes closed. . . .

The soft chime of a bell drew her from dreamlessness.

"Arianna," came a soft, sweet voice.

Arianna raised her head. She wasn't sitting by the campfire. She was in a velvety darkness that lapped around her shoulders like a cloak.

"Arianna!" The voice was closer. A soft breath whispered past her ear. She smelled flowers.

"Atalanta?"

The Dreamspeaker took shape before her. Her crystal horn was dim and the soft lavender of her coat was bleached to a cottony white. Only her violet eyes glowed brightly in her ghostly face.

"Atalanta!" Arianna cried. "I've missed you so much!" She fumbled for the Scepter, then held it triumphantly aloft. "Chase and I got the Scepter back!"

"Wonderful," the violet mare said.

Ari strained forward. "I can't hear you, Dreamspeaker! Can you hear me? Chase and I got the Scepter back. Only I don't know exactly how to use the magic. There are some parts of its magic I recall very well. But I had just passed the first stage of my training with the Scepter, hadn't I? I was to learn more as I grew older — but then, the Shifter came —"

30

"Shifter . . ." the ghostly voice whispered.

"And then my training was interrupted. I must know more, Dreamspeaker," Ari implored.

". . . Indigo Star," Atalanta said. The vision of her shimmered in the night. Her long silver mane stirred about her withers. "Eliane Bohnes . . . we are fading . . . fading. . . ."

Her voice trailed away. Her image shimmered once more — and was gone.

Ari awoke with a start. The campfire burned low, red embers snapping in the cool air. A thumbnail moon hung low in the sky. She could make out the dim shapes of Finn and Lori, two separate rolls of blankets on the opposite side of the fire. Lincoln roused himself and nudged her hand with his nose.

Ari rose to her feet. With Lincoln padding behind her, she picked her way through the grass to where Chase, Toby, and Rednal were asleep for the night.

The Sunchaser was awake and moving toward her before she reached the unicorns. Ari reached up and flung her arms around his neck. She buried her nose in his mane. He smelled of wild grass and fresh air.

"Something is wrong in the Celestial Valley," she said.

"Yes," Chase answered.

Ari sighed. Chase always knew.

"Ask the Scepter," he said.

Ari squinted at him. She could barely make

31

out his features in the dark. The whites of his eyes caught a stray beam of moonlight. "Of course," she said. "I'm not thinking straight." She pulled the Scepter from among the folds of her skirt and held it up. "Scepter?"

The unicorn head swiveled toward them both. The rosewood shaft began to glow.

"I could not hear the Dreamspeaker when she came to me," Ari said. "Is there a reason for this?"

"It's dark," the wooden head replied.

"I know it's dark. It's nighttime. But why can't I hear Atalanta?"

"The magic is dark," the Scepter said. "Something is blocking the Deep Magic."

"But we passed the trial by fire and the ordeal by moonlight," Ari said. "The balance of magic should be equal again."

The Scepter didn't answer. Ari bit her lip in exasperation. Of course it wouldn't answer. She had to ask the Scepter a question.

"Why can't I hear Atalanta?"

But no matter how many times she asked, or how many ways she asked, the carved head only replied, "The magic is dark."

Finally, Ari gave up. She resisted the impulse to whack the Scepter against a large tree to knock some sense into it. She ran her hands through her hair. Chase snorted sympathetically.

"What do you think we should do now?" said Ari.

"I don't know, milady. Perhaps Dr. Bohnes has the answer."

"I hope she does," Ari said a little grimly. "We have to talk to her right away."

They were up early the next morning. The sky was clear and the air was fresh. Ari's fears of the night before receded in the light of the beautiful day. She would find Dr. Bohnes, and she would have a simple answer that would tell her why Atalanta couldn't get through Ari's dreams.

The whole party set off with a light heart. The closer Ari came to Balinor Village and the Unicorn Inn, the more determined she grew. She would take back her kingdom from the Shifter! She would find her family again!

Finally, they came into the outskirts of the village.

Ari was amazed at how much she missed Balinor. How good she felt to be back!

Life in Balinor was not at all like life on the other side of the Gap. At Glacier River Farm, life had been quiet and simple, but the big city, only a few miles away, had been loud and hectic, filled with the stink of gasoline and the smell of exhaust.

In Balinor, there were no cars or buses. No huge steel buildings or streetlights. No hard pavement under her feet. Balinor was strewn with peaceful fields and flowers. Homes were small and pretty. There was a daily market in the middle of town where farmers bought and sold fruits and vegetables, and where people traded pottery, handmade clothes, wooden tools, and other wares.

And, of course, there were the unicorns of Balinor. They were not immortal, like their Celestial brothers and sisters. But the unicorns were all different.

The Workers were strong and proud, with thick, hard, bony horns and stout, muscular bodies. They pulled wagons and plows. The Warriors were huge and powerful. Their horns were like iron and were as long as a walking stick.

The Royals were a separate breed, with beautiful jewels at the base of their horns and lean, athletic bodies. Those unicorns lived at the Royal Palace and in the great halls of the Seven Lords of Balinor. After the day of the Great Betrayal, the Palace unicorns had scattered. Ari hadn't seen one since she'd returned to Balinor. She feared that when the Shifter captured and imprisoned her parents, he had captured and imprisoned the Royal unicorns as well.

And then there were the Celestial unicorns, like Sunchaser, Rednal, and Toby. They were tall, strong, muscular, and athletic — all at once. And the jewels at the base of their horns held magic — their own personal magic. Their visits to Balinor from the Celestial Valley above were few and far between. They only appeared when they were bonded to a human or in times of crisis, during great events and wars.

Such as the one they were about to fight, Ari feared.

She ran one hand along Chase's muscular neck. She bent forward and whispered, "I'm glad to be home."

"And I am, too, milady." He curvetted in the road, the dust puffing up beneath his hooves. Chase, too, would regain his kingdom, Ari vowed to herself. Chase was Lord of the Animals in Balinor. The special bond between them made possible what Ari loved most about her land: that all the animals could talk. It was one of the things that made this world peaceful and special.

It was one of the things the Shifter, if he had his way, would ruin with his evil magic.

"The sky has opened up and smiled upon the world!" a loud voice shouted. "Can this day be so special? Can it be true? Is it — is it?"

Ari drew Chase to a halt and climbed down. They were in front of the Unicorn Inn, and Samlett himself came running out of the door. He was carrying two large buckets of water. He tried to run with them for a few steps, but the buckets were clearly slowing him down, so he dropped them without ceremony and they splashed onto the dirt road. "It *is* you!" He looked as if he might cry. "*Princess Arianna*," he said dramatically, bowing low and sweeping his arm across his large, round body. "Permission to hug you, I say, to hug you."

Ari couldn't help but smile. "Permission granted." Laughing, they gave each other a big hug. Everyone was happy to see old Samlett, too.

"They say your mission was successful, milady." Samlett beamed hopefully at her from behind his large mustache. "Dr. Bohnes had word from the Dreamspeaker herself, two days ago."

"She did? But how . . . ?" Ari stopped herself. If the Dreamspeaker had reached Dr. Bohnes, then there had to be some simple explanation about why, as the Scepter said, "the magic was dark."

She needed to talk to her old nurse. "Is Dr. Bohnes here, in Balinor?" she asked Samlett.

"No, Your Royal Highness. She was called to Luckon. She will be back as soon as she can. Only an emergency would take her from your side." He heaved a happy sigh. "So! Your mission was successful, milady? You have . . ." He leaned forward, and his round face gleamed with excitement. "You have . . . it?"

"Yes," she said after a pause. "Our mission was successful. We have recovered the Royal Scepter." And she drew the Scepter out from her vest and held it in the air. The rosewood shaft gleamed softly in the dusk. The unicorn head gazed straight ahead with its lapis lazuli eyes.

Samlett stared at the rosewood staff in Ari's

hand with an expression of awe. "The Scepter?" he whispered.

"Of course I'm the Royal Scepter," the unicorn head replied. "What do I look like — a frog's leg?"

Samlett jumped back. "And it talks, too! Isn't that something, I say something?"

"Of course it's something," the unicorn head answered. "It's also obvious to anyone with half a brain."

Ari laughed. "I'm sorry, Samlett. The first thing you'll learn about the Royal Scepter is not to ask any questions in front of it unless you really need to hear the answer."

"Yes, well, I can see that," Samlett said. "Anyway, I'm so happy that you and His Majesty have returned safely." He bowed again to Chase, who lowered his horn in return. "I knew you could do it, Princess. I knew you could beat the Shifter at his own game. Trial by fire and ordeal by moonlight — *pfaaaw*! You showed him, I say showed him!"

"Yes, she did!" Finn remarked.

Samlett looked at Finn curiously, as if noticing him for the first time.

"Hello to you, too," Lori said to Samlett, stepping forward.

"Oh, yes, good to see you, my child."

"I'm not your child. And this is Finn. Without

Finn's help, Ari never would have beaten the Shifter," Lori said smugly.

"It's true," Ari said. "When I was in desperate need, Finn was there to help me."

Finn ran one hand through his red hair and blushed. "I'm just grateful Rednal and I had the chance to help Her Royal Highness."

"Well," Samlett said, "all that matters is that the day was won. You're all to be thanked. And a celebration is in order. Come — come inside the Inn. A feast, I say a feast! My wife, Runetta, and I will make a feast fit for my Princess! And for you unicorns, the finest, I say the finest hay and oats in the stable!"

Ari followed Chase, Toby, and Rednal to the unicorn barn to see them comfortably settled. Lori, Samlett, and Lincoln went inside the Inn. Finn stood awkwardly, looking after Ari and the unicorns, then toward the Inn. Finally, he broke into a run and came up to Ari just as she was bringing Chase a large bucket of oats.

"Your Highness!" His face was red. His breath came unevenly.

"Yes, Finn." Ari kept her voice casual. She set the oats in front of Chase, then picked a comb out of his saddlebag and ran it through his glossy mane. "Let me do that for you."

"I'm the only one who takes care of Chase," Ari said firmly.

"But Your Royal Highness!"

Ari set the comb on the stall floor. Samlett's

unicorn stalls were large and comfortable. Mirrors hung on the walls, and the floor was thick with clean, sweet straw. Ari nudged the straw aside with one toe of her boot. It was time to settle things with Finn. "Are you going to continue calling me 'Your Royal Highness'?"

Finn had a wash of freckles across his nose. He turned pale and they stood out in stark contrast with his skin. "Am I wrong in the way I'm addressing you, milady?"

"Yes," Ari said. "I want you to call me Ari."

"But! Your Royal Highness . . . I can't!"

"You must." Ari took a step nearer to Finn. He stepped back nervously. "I won't bite. I'm the same person you helped out of the surf after the ordeal by moonlight. The same person who went swimming with you and Rednal. And you weren't embarrassed to be around me then."

"I didn't know then," he said hoarsely. "I didn't know you were Princess Arianna!"

"Well, you know now. So what? Are you going to keep Your-Royal-Highnessing me while we're gathering the Resistance to fight the Shifter?"

"Well . . . yes."

"Oh." Ari tugged at a piece of her hair. "Why?"

"Because I am not your equal, milady." Finn scrubbed the toe of his boot in the straw.

"Of course you are!" she said, astonished. "We all have different jobs to do, Finn. Mr. Samlett's is to run the Inn. Dr. Bohnes cares for the sick. And I have to be a leader. We all have different jobs, but we're all worth the same!"

"What is *my* job?" Finn asked. "I'm from a poor village on the other side of the sea. I've never been out of Deridia until now. I've never known a time when the Shifter and his shadow unicorns didn't roam the streets. My job is to clean the stable at my parents' Inn, and since I've left there I don't have even that job anymore."

"I'll give you a job," Ari said recklessly.

"You will?"

"Yes." She thought a moment. "You can be . . ."

"A cavalry captain," Chase suggested.

Ari clapped her hands. "Perfect!"

Chase nodded. "And Rednal, too, milady. The pair of them would be fit to lead any charge against the Shifter."

"A captain of the cavalry!" Finn said. He grinned. "I like the sound of that."

"So do I," Ari said. "And so I dub you . . . Finn, captain of the Royal Cavalry, which, at the moment, consists of the two of you — Rednal and Finn!"

"We'll fix that," Finn said with confidence. "I can recruit more riders and their unicorns! Soon we will have an army!" He looked her in the eye. "Thanks, Your Roy — I mean, milady."

"Well, *that's* taken care of," Ari said with a sigh of relief. "Now let's get something to eat!"

The Unicorn Inn was warm and cozy. A small fire crackled in the fireplace. They all sat at a round table in the main hall. Only a few people were at the Inn this night, and they were seated far away from them.

Samlett served tall, cool drinks to the party — spring water flavored with lemon and lime. Ari could smell the food cooking and this made her realize how terribly hungry she was. She hadn't been able to eat anything during the storm on the *Dawnwalker.*

Ari placed the Royal Scepter in the corner, where she could see it, but far enough away so that it wouldn't answer every question asked at the table.

Finally, Samlett and his wife, Runetta, served a wonderful meal of sweet cakes, spiced vegetables, cinnamon apples, pies, and bread. They all sat down together and ate hungrily.

Runetta was a beautiful, gracious woman with white hair and the smoothest skin Ari had ever seen. She was as big around her middle as her husband, Samlett, but a lot more graceful. "Now that the Princess has safely returned with the Royal Scepter," she said, "I think we all need to talk about something."

"Like what?" said Lori, swallowing a huge bite of sweet cake. "I don't want to hear any more about that Shifter and how we have to conquer him

41

or whatever. I've been to his lousy castle, and I'm not going back."

"What we need to talk about," Runetta said kindly, "is a formal ceremony in which we present the Royal Scepter to its rightful owner, the only current ruling member of the Royal Family — the Princess Arianna."

Everyone stopped eating all at once. Ari didn't know what to say. "But . . . but," she stammered.

"Runetta is right, milady!" Samlett proclaimed, pounding his fist on the table so heavily that the plates and silverware jumped. "I hadn't thought of it myself, although I should have, I say I should have."

"Why would you want to do that?" Finn asked. "I thought Ari needed to hide from the Shifter."

"Yeah," said Lori. "Are you guys crazy or something?"

"No, Runetta's right." Samlett wiped pie crumbs from his chin with a cloth napkin. "Tell them what you're thinking, Runetta."

Runetta smiled and held her husband's hand. "Well, we knew there would come a time when we would want everyone in the world to know that the Princess Arianna had returned. We just couldn't let everyone know she had returned while the Shifter held the Royal Scepter."

"But isn't that dangerous?" asked Lincoln.

"Aren't there a lot of spies still loyal to the Shifter who would want to capture or hurt Ari?"

"Yes," said Samlett, his eyes narrowing. "It's a risk. There are still plenty of evil forces out there loyal to the Shifter. But there are even more people loyal to the Princess and the Royal Family."

Runetta nodded eagerly. "Yes, yes, and if they knew that the Princess was back in Balinor and she had regained the Scepter, we could get more people on our side who were no longer afraid to show their support. It might be a risk worth taking."

"I see," said Finn. "There's more people *for* the Princess than against her. So if we give the people their Princess, if we offer everybody hope —"

Samlett stood up and shook his fist. "We'll get rid of the Shifter once and for all!"

"Quiet, dear," said Runetta, glancing around the room. "You never know who's listening." There were only a few people around, none of them close enough to hear their conversation, but Runetta was a wise woman.

"Oops, sorry, dear." Samlett sat down again. "I got a little carried away, I say carried away. My apologies, Your Royal Highness."

"No need to apologize. We all want to defeat the Shifter."

And that's what it came down to, Ari knew. She would have to do whatever it took to drive the Shifter out of this world forever. She would have to do whatever it took to restore her parents to the throne and bring peace and justice back to the people and the land that she loved. And if that meant taking risks — well, she was getting used to that.

Runetta stood and cut a big piece of sweet potato pie. "Of course, it's Princess Arianna's decision. No one else can make up her mind for her. And it's an important decision. Think about it today and sleep on it tonight. We can discuss the plan again tomorrow." She put the pie on Finn's plate and patted his head. "You're getting a hot bath and a good scrubbing this afternoon, young man."

"Thank you, ma'am," Finn said, digging into the pie.

"Well, I think it's a bad idea and a big deal over nothing," said Lori. "If everybody in the world starts calling Ari 'Princess' and bowing at her feet . . . it's stupid."

Ari raised her eyebrows. "I'd be glad to hand the job over to you, Lori — Shifter, shadow unicorns, and all."

Lori scowled, opened her mouth to reply, then thought better of it.

They ate the rest of their meal happily, talking about other things — the season's harvest and the feed delivery for the stables and the firewood that the boy hadn't chopped yet — and Ari lost herself in the warmth of friendship that filled the room. But the thought of being Princess never completely left her mind.

The responsibility kept mounting. The stakes kept rising. If she allowed Runetta to hold a formal ceremony announcing that she — the Princess Arianna — had returned to Balinor, things would never be the same for her. She might never be free again.

The very first thing she had to do was see Dr. Bohnes and, through her, talk to Atalanta. She would leave to find her old friend tomorrow.

6

The group at the Unicorn Inn stayed up late that night talking and laughing. Ari checked on Chase one last time before she went to bed, then went up to the room Runetta had prepared for her. Samlett's wife had decorated the bed with her finest velvet bedspread. Bowls of fragrant flowers were placed in every corner. A fire burned softly in the stone fireplace to keep the evening chill from the air.

But Ari couldn't sleep. She sat on the window seat and looked out at the shining stars. She let her mind wander. When she wasn't thinking too hard, memories of her life before came back.

She remembered a day when her brother Bren taught her how to use a sword. They were in the courtyard. "Hold it like this," he had said, wrapping his large hand gently over her tiny fingers and adjusting them around the hilt of the sword. "And when you stand, stand perfectly sideways."

She remembered learning how to ride the Royal unicorns bareback. She must have only been three or four years old, but she remembered her first ride on Xavier, a small, sleek, and gentle unicorn. The jewel at the base of his horn was an amber star. She remembered hanging on for dear life when Xavier had decided — quite suddenly — to chase a butterfly across an open field. All the stable boys chased madly after them, shouting, "Whoa! Whoa! Xavier! Whoa!"

She remembered her first trip to the marketplace, when she understood for the very first time that not everyone lived in the Royal Palace. "Most people," her mother, the Queen, had told her, "farm their crops, raise animals, and weave their own clothing. They get up in the morning and work the land, draw milk from the cows and goats, churn butter and cheese, cook their own meals, and go to bed at night exhausted from their labors. It's important for you to understand how our people live, so that when the time comes to serve them, you will serve them well."

The Queen, of course, had been right. Now it was time for Princess Arianna to serve her people, to give them hope, to lead them well. It didn't matter if it was hard work. It didn't matter if it was dangerous. Being a member of the Royal Family was not just a privilege. She had a duty to the people to pre-serve their way of life and protect them against the threat of evil.

The stars seemed to be smiling at her, so Ari smiled back. "Maybe I'm not meant to live an ordi-nary life," she told the stars. "Maybe I'm meant to be a Princess. And maybe it doesn't bother me any-more."

7

O n the third day after the Shifter's theft of the Indigo Star, the sun rose sullenly over the Valley of Fear. Far away in Balinor, Ari slept with her dog, Lincoln, at her side.

In the Valley of Fear, fetid smoke from the pits in the Fiery Field tainted the air. The desolate desert lay quiet.

A lone light shone in the north tower of Castle Entia. The Shifter paced back and forth across the granite floor. His iron hooves clanked like the strikes of an iron hammer. His red eyes were gaunt. He watched the dawn creep over Demonview.

A weak, red sun sent one ray across the valley.

"Now I must go," the Shifter said to no one. He was alone inside Castle Entia. He preferred to be alone.

The Shifter, with the powerful magic of the

Indigo Star, felt the great dragon Naytin rise from its sleep many miles away, deep inside Blue Mountain.

The Shifter lowered his head and concentrated on using his shifting magic. He grew a human arm from his thickly muscled chest. He had tied the Indigo Star around his neck with a length of silken rope. Now he took the Indigo Star off and carefully laid it in a magic box, casting a spell of protection over it. It pained him to leave it behind.

"This will be the last time I will ever be without you," he said to the Star, the source of his new and mighty magic. "But if I am going to talk to the dragon, the foul beast must not suspect that I have stolen its precious stone."

The Shifter sprouted wings and leaped out of the castle tower. With two strong beats in the air, he was flying at an incredible speed, soaring out over the Forest of Ardit. Aided by the strength of his new magic, each powerful stroke carried him effortlessly for miles.

The Shifter could feel the dragon's anger rising. The beast was fully awake now.

He beat his wings twice more and landed upon a gentle rise overlooking Pearl Lake, at the foot of Blue Mountain. If what he had heard about the dragon was true, the beast would plunge into Pearl Lake to feed on the weeds and fish. After years of sleep, Naytin would have only enough strength to reach the water and eat. Then the dragon would seek its revenge against whoever had stolen the Indigo Star.

The Shifter began to transform his body from that of a winged unicorn into a gray wolf. He made the wolf old and haggard, with tired eyes and matted fur.

Then he saw the dragon burst forth from the mountain, sending tons of shattered rock and hundreds of uprooted trees into the air. Birds and animals darted away, screeching in terror. Stones and dust fell in the dragon's wake as the beast spread out its wings, which blocked the sun. The Shifter cringed in fear at the horrible cry that came from somewhere deep within Naytin's lungs.

And then the dragon pitched sharply toward the earth and plunged into Pearl Lake, splashing thousands of gallons of water out across the mountain range.

For a long time, the dragon remained underwater, but finally the beast emerged, its silvery hide glittering in the sun, its belly fat and full. Remnants of weeds and fish fell from its gigantic jaws. It stepped out of the lake and growled — the sound of ten thousand angry bears.

The Shifter ignored his fear and loped down the rise to stand before the dragon. He was so small next to the dragon that Naytin didn't even notice him.

"Dragon!" shouted the Shifter. "Oh, great dragon!"

Naytin glanced down at him, blinking its watery eyes. "Go away, wolf. I have no time for you. Someone has stolen my Indigo Star, and I will tear apart the land tree by tree until I find who is responsible."

"But dragon," said the Shifter, "that is exactly why I have come. I know who stole your Star."

The dragon screamed. The sound rose up like a tornado against the azure sides of Blue Mountain. Naytin stretched, fully extending itself, flexing its monstrous wings high above its head. "Speak, wolf! Tell me what you know!"

"Yes, great one. Although I am nothing but an old gray wolf, my eyes are still strong, and I am wise like my brothers and sisters."

"I know the wolves. You are keen hunters. You see things and know things that other animals do not. Speak truthfully now or I will crush you into the ground and leave you for the crows."

"Yes, great one," the Shifter said. "Only two days ago I watched a band of humans walk the trail to the foot of Blue Mountain. I was curious about them because they did not look like hunters, and they did not look like warriors."

"Who were they, then?"

"They were thieves, great dragon."

"THIEVES!" cried Naytin with such horrible anger that the Shifter wanted to howl with joy. He laid his gray forepaw over his snout to hide his joy. His plan was almost complete.

"How do you know this?" demanded the dragon.

Entia blinked his yellow eyes innocently. "One night, when their fire was low, I crept close to their camp. I listened to their words."

"What did they say, wolf? Tell me!" The great dragon lowered its head and looked directly into Entia's eyes. The Shifter could feel Naytin's hot breath against his furry face.

"I heard one of the men say, 'The Indigo Star will soon be ours.'"

"NOOOO!" the dragon lifted its head and shrieked at the sky. "What else? What else did they say?"

"They said they would bring the Star back to the Village of Balinor and be rich forever. They said that the dragon would never know — that you had lost your power. They said that you were no longer a beast to be feared."

The dragon leaped into the air and soared high above Blue Mountain, screeching with rage.

The Shifter sat down and curled his tail around his feet. His red tongue lolled in satisfaction. He raised his head and howled his joy to the skies. He saw a great shadow eclipse the sun, and then he looked up and watched the vast underbelly of the dragon pass overhead. The beast was on its way to take its revenge on Balinor.

Entia waited until the thunderous sound of Naytin's passing faded.

53

Then he began to laugh. A laugh filled with darkness and hate and the knowledge of his evil victory.

The Indigo Star was his. He had more power and magic than he had ever known before. Soon the dragon would destroy the Village of Balinor. The Resistance would be broken. All he need do now was capture the Princess and that bronze beast, the Sunchaser. He would regain the Royal Scepter. No one could stop him then! He was only one small step away from total victory.

He would rule this land, and all would bow before him.

Even the Celestial unicorns!

8

Far away, in Balinor Village, Ari woke to a dull sun. Lincoln was curled fast asleep in the corner. She rose quietly, then sat at the low window for a moment. It was early and the village still slept. There was something strange about the sky. Ari wrapped her arms around herself and shivered a little. She felt a sudden longing for Dr. Bohnes. She and Chase needed help. She would leave right after lunch, no matter how much Runetta and Samlett wanted to announce her presence to all of Balinor.

What had happened to her happy mood of the night before? Ari jumped up, determined not to let the dreary day affect her spirits. She washed in the bowl of water Runetta had left on the simple wooden dresser, then pinned her bronze hair in a knot on the top of her head. She looked at herself in the small mirror over the dresser. There were dark circles under her eyes; they looked more gray than blue this morning.

An early morning gallop would cheer her up. Should she take the Royal Scepter? She had tucked it in the large chest at the foot of the bed, underneath the few clothes she carried with her. The Scepter would be safe there. Safer than attached to her belt, where someone from the village might recognize the rosewood shaft and the lapis lazuli unicorn head.

Careful not to wake the sleeping collie, she dressed hastily in breeches and boots, then slipped downstairs to the kitchen. She took a peach for herself and an apple for Chase, then went to look for her unicorn.

The day outside was warmer than Ari had expected. A wind was rising. Chase was as uneasy as she was, and agreed that a good stiff gallop would clear their minds. She decided against a saddle and bridle. Chase knelt down and she jumped onto his bare back.

They trotted easily down the deserted street that ran down the middle of the village. A few shopkeepers were stirring, and Ari raised a hand in greeting. Most waved back. A few straightened up and stared after her.

It was becoming more and more difficult for her to disguise the truth of her identity. How long could she pretend that Chase was just a regular unicorn? His height and strength and bearing were remarkable. Sooner or later, someone would put it all together — the Scepter — a Celestial unicorn — the Royal Princess!

In the open meadows surrounding Balinor, the place where she, Lori, and Lincoln had been flung from the Gap, she opened Chase up. He stretched his long legs and raced as fast as he had run in the trial by fire. Ari bent over his neck. Her hair came undone and mingled with his flying mane. It was almost impossible to tell the two colors apart.

After their run, Ari brushed Chase in the stables behind Samlett's small Inn. Toby and Rednal were already up and about, grazing in the paddock filled with fresh green grass Samlett kept for unicorns. Ari nodded greetings to the stable hand mucking out the stalls, but didn't speak. Somehow, it didn't seem the right kind of morning for conversation. She sent a mental message to Chase, *Let's not speak aloud this morning. I don't know who will overhear us.*

As usual, Chase picked up on her mood.

Is it true, what Lincoln told me? Chase thought to her.

Is what true?

You know what I'm thinking about. Are Samlett and Runetta going to hold a formal ceremony and announce that you're the Princess?

The wind blew heavily against the stables and sent loose hay swirling through the stalls. Ari slipped the currycomb back into her saddlebag and leaned against Chase with a sigh. *I know it sounds dangerous, Chase, but we can't keep it a secret forever. Besides, the time might be right. The Shifter's power is weakening. If we could organize a strong force now, we just might be able to march on the Castle Entia and defeat him. If the people know that I am back in Balinor and that I have regained the Royal Scepter, they will fight for me. I know they will.*

Chase blew gently into her hair. *An announcement seems a little premature to me. That's the way humans are, you know, always so eager to get into trouble. They love big ceremonies and grand gestures. We don't know how powerful the Shifter is. Just because you've got the Scepter and you won the trial by fire and the ordeal by moonlight doesn't mean the Shifter is helpless. He has spent a lot of time and effort building up a strong army, and the forces of evil are not so easily defeated.*

I know, Chase, but there is something to be said for striking quickly, for pressing our advantage. It's so difficult to know what to do. I wish . . . I wish . . .

What, milady?

I wish my mother was here. She's so wise, Chase. She would know what to do.

Perhaps we will know after Dr. Bohnes helps us speak to Atalanta.

Ari nodded. *I hope so. But I've been thinking,*

Chase. I need to start making my own decisions. I need to start acting like the Princess.

Suddenly, the wind kicked up even stronger. The stable doors banged against their posts, an empty bucket went rattling across the floor, and Ari felt her hair swirl around her head. "I don't like this wind," she said aloud. "I think there's a storm rising."

As if in answer, the storm came in full.

A terrible wind ripped the barn doors off their hinges and sent wooden planks flying into the air.

Chase reared and whinnied, a long, clarion call. In the distance, Rednal and Toby whinnied back.

Ari shouted, "We've got to get out of this wind!"

Samlett dashed into the stables shouting, "Princess!"

"Samlett!" she cried. "What's happening?"

"Storm!" Samlett shouted. The wind whipped his mustache against his cheeks. His eyes were watering as the dust flew into them. "Quick, follow me to the fruit cellar!"

Ari turned to Chase. "I'm not leaving Chase."

"You have no choice!" Samlett yelled. "If we don't go now, we could both be killed, I say killed."

The wind was so strong it howled and whistled through the stable, nearly pulling Ari off her feet. She shook her head. Was the Innkeeper crazy? Leave Chase?

Go, milady! I will not have you risk your life for me!

"No, Chase, I won't leave you."

"Samlett, TAKE HER!" Chase reared and sprang away. Ari lunged after him.

"Forgive me, Princess," Samlett said. Then he grabbed Ari's arm and yanked her away.

"No!" Ari tried to pull against him, but Samlett had a surprisingly firm grip. And the wind — the wind was so strong she could barely stand. She squinted against its fury. Chase had leaped the fence into the paddock. He was herding Toby and Rednal before him. His ebony horn flashed in the dim sunlight.

"Chase!" Ari screamed. She struggled furiously with Samlett. He pulled her across the yard. Runetta, Finn, Lori, and Lincoln were already at the fruit cellar. The three humans were struggling with the door.

Dirt and tools and chickens were being flung around the Inn's courtyard. The gale was so strong it stole her breath. She gasped as Samlett pushed her toward the doors of the fruit cellar.

Ari looked up at the sky. The sun was shrouded by a shadow. The shadow was so huge she couldn't take it all in at once. She saw a wing, and another, and then a tail as long as Glacier River. What was it? "Samlett!" She pointed to the sky. Her mind finally put everything together into a complete picture.

A huge dragon! She knew it was the dragon Naytin, circling overhead. She remembered her father, the King, telling stories of a mammoth beast that lived in Blue Mountain and guarded the Indigo Star — a dragon that had slept for years — for lifetimes — without waking. She remembered her father saying that the dragon's breath was so strong it could blow hurricanes across the land. Naytin was up there, and it was blowing hurricanes!

"Don't stop, Princess, please!" Samlett pushed Ari forward.

Ari put down her head and pushed against the wind. Even with Samlett behind her, she could barely make headway. "We'll never make it!" she shouted.

The dragon screeched. It was a horrible, ear-splitting shriek that shook the very earth beneath Ari's feet. She glanced up and saw Naytin swoop low over Balinor Village — so low that she could feel the heat of its immense body. Then the beast soared upward again, as straight and graceful as an arrow shot into the sky.

Finally, they reached the fruit cellar. Samlett, still refusing to let go of Ari, reached down and pulled open the cellar door.

Runetta, Lori, Finn, and Lincoln were already down inside the underground storage basement, along with all of the other people from

Samlett's staff at the Inn. Ari went inside with Samlett right behind her. Runetta took Ari in her arms. The door slammed shut, and Samlett bolted it closed with an iron bar.

Everyone gathered around Ari. "You made it!" said Finn.

"We were all worried," Lincoln said, nuzzling against Ari's leg.

Ari bent down and hugged her dog.

"Oh, Samlett," Runetta said. "I was so worried about you . . . I think I'm going to cry —"

"There, there," said Samlett. He embraced Runetta and gently patted her back. "Everything is all right now. The Princess and I are safe, I say safe."

"But what about Chase?" said Ari.

Suddenly, she heard Chase scream in her mind. It was so horrible she fell to her knees. "Oh, no, Chase!" But the connection to his mind was gone. She couldn't find him. "Chase!"

Ari ran past everyone, up the stairs of the fruit cellar. Samlett and Runetta grabbed her before she could reach the door. "Easy, my child," Runetta said in her comforting voice. "The Sunchaser will be all right. There is nothing you can do for him."

"I can't let him . . . I can't let him be alone out there in that wind. He might be hurt."

"Milady." Samlett turned her around sharply and looked into her eyes. "If you go out there in that hurricane, you might be killed. You can't afford to die. You're too important in the fight against the Shifter. You don't have just yourself or the Sunchaser to think about now. From this day forward, you must think about your people."

The fruit cellar had become eerily quiet. Not a sound could be heard, except for the fierce winds howling outside, rattling the wooden door against its iron bar.

Ari's heart was torn in two: She was Ari! And she had to save Chase!

But she wasn't just Ari. She was the Princess Arianna. She had a duty to help her people.

Didn't Samlett know that all she could think about since this whole thing began, since she first returned from the other side of the Gap, was that she was the Princess and nothing would ever be easy for her again? She would have to battle the Shifter and rally the forces of good against evil and pretend, pretend, PRETEND she was strong, when all she really wanted to do was cry. Ari felt suddenly cold and alone.

It was Lori's voice that broke the chill. "Honestly, Ari. Samlett's right, you know. You can't go out there. Even I know that. I would have made a much better Princess than you. Are you sure there hasn't been some mistake? Maybe it really is *me*, I mean, you know, like I'm the *real* Princess. Has anybody looked into that?"

Everyone laughed — Samlett and Runetta

and all the people who worked at the Inn. Even Lincoln and Finn and Ari chuckled. The laughter echoed in the fruit cellar and felt warm and friendly.

"It's not that funny!" Lori snapped angrily. "I just don't understand you people." She stormed off into a corner.

Finn chased after her. "Don't be upset. Look how you've cheered everyone up," Finn said kindly.

Lori turned around. Ari expected to see Lori's aggravated, self-involved pout, but instead Lori was smiling.

"Not everyone can have a positive effect on people," Lori said smartly. "It takes a great deal of talent."

Finn sat next to Lori on an overturned bushel basket.

Lincoln scratched busily at one tuliped ear. "That boy is truly remarkable."

"Princess," said Samlett, clasping her shoulders. "Listen. The winds have died down."

Ari hesitated only a moment until she understood what Samlett was saying, then she flung herself up the steps.

Samlett helped her pull back the iron bar and push open the heavy door. She climbed quickly out of the fruit cellar and looked all around. She couldn't believe the destruction she saw.

Fences were leveled. Trees were uprooted, their branches snapped and littered all over the ground like kindling wood. Homes and stables were laid to waste, their roofs and tables and chairs and barn tools broken and strewn across the land. Animals were everywhere, some standing alone and confused in the fields, some fallen and hurt, others running around terrified. People began slowly, silently emerging from their underground cellars.

Ari ran out to the road, desperately searching for the Sunchaser. *Chase! Chase! Where are you? Please, talk to me!*

I'm all right, Princess, but perhaps you'd better come to me.

Where are you? I'll come right away.

I don't know where I am. I was blown around and now I'm stuck.

Stuck? I'll find you, Chase, don't worry.

But it was Tobiano who found the Sunchaser. "Princess! Here! Over here!" he shouted. "I've found the Sunchaser. You won't believe this."

Ari ran toward Toby, relieved that he was safe, too. The unicorn was around the far side of the Inn. When she reached him, she couldn't believe her eyes.

Chase was safe all right, but his horn was buried deep in the trunk of a huge oak tree that hadn't been toppled by the dragon's hurricane.

"I'm stuck," he said in a frustrated voice. "I can't pull my horn free."

Toby started laughing. "I've never seen anything like it before."

Lori, Finn, Samlett, and Runetta came and

laughed, too. Soon, everyone was laughing, even Ari, just like in the fruit cellar. Ari knew why she was laughing. She was so relieved that Chase was all right, if she didn't laugh she would cry.

"I'm glad that you've all had a good chuckle," Chase said, clearly annoyed. "Now maybe you can get me out of here."

Ari ran up to Chase and hugged his neck. "Don't worry, my friend. We'll get you out. I promise." She stroked his mane and kissed his ears.

"The dragon's breath picked me up off my hooves and blew me across Samlett's field. The wind sent me headfirst into this oak tree. It's a good thing, too, or I might have been blown all the way back to Sixton."

"Oh, Chase," Ari said. "I never should have left you."

"Nonsense. We did the right thing. You're not as strong as I am. You might have been seriously hurt in the hurricane, and I might have been hurt trying to protect you."

Samlett and two of his workers returned with an ax and an auger, and they gouged a hole in the tree large enough for Sunchaser to pull out his horn. The mighty unicorn shook out his mane and stretched his neck.

Ari rested her hand on Chase's back and inspected him. He had bruises on his legs and a nasty brush burn on his hindquarters. "Let me take care of those wounds right away."

"There's nothing you can do," Chase said. "They'll heal on their own. Besides, there are more important things for you to tend to." He surveyed the landscape. "I can't believe the damage that dragon caused."

"This is serious business," Samlett said. "We'll need to have an emergency meeting of the Resistance right away."

"The Resistance?" said Ari. "Why?"

It was Runetta who answered. "There is a reason the dragon has left its lair again after so long. Someone must have stolen the Indigo Star. And there can be only one being sly and evil enough to have done it."

"The Indigo Star?" Lori said. "What the heck is that?"

Ari knew — Ari *remembered*. "It's the most powerful magical talisman in all the land. And if the Shifter has it . . ."

Sunchaser snorted. Lincoln growled. Samlett grunted. Finn made a groaning sound.

"What? What?" Lori asked.

"If the Shifter has it," Ari said, "it changes everything."

She closed her eyes and bit her lip. So that was what the Scepter had meant. The Indigo Star was in the hands of the Shifter.

And the Scepter's own magic was blocked!

9

"We will not," Ari said a few hours later, "announce my return right now."

"I agree," Runetta said. Samlett had called a meeting of the villagers after the dragon storm. They were ready to go downstairs to greet them. Ari had canceled her plans to go to Dr. Bohnes. She was needed here.

"The Shifter's power is immense, now that he has the Indigo Star," Samlett said. His large kind face was creased with worry. "The fewer people who know who you are, the safer you'll be from his clutches."

"Then we're agreed," Lincoln said. "Let's go downstairs. They're waiting for us."

The large, wood-planked great room of Samlett's Inn was packed full of frightened villagers. Ari sat cramped together at a side table with Lori, Lincoln, and Finn, near the door to the kitchen. Samlett and Runetta sat at the head table with other leaders of the Resistance.

Ari leaned back against the wall and closed her eyes. Even the Shifter wasn't safe with Naytin on the rampage. She wondered if Entia knew what kind of power he had unleashed when he'd stolen the Star. He would have to remain at Castle Entia until Naytin's reign of terror was over and the giant dragon went back to Blue Mountain for another thousand-year sleep — and it wouldn't do that until it found the Star.

All had been chaos after Naytin's attack on the village. Ari had helped Samlett and the others clear the paved courtyard of debris. The unicorns returned to the paddock. A few of the servants in Samlett's household had suffered cuts and bruises, and Ari helped bind their wounds. The villagers emerged slowly from their homes after the dragon storm, then gathered at the Inn to decide what to do.

"There's only one reason the dragon attacked Balinor, and we all know what it is!" proclaimed a fat man with a full, thick beard the color of sand. He stood up and addressed the room in a razor-sharp voice. "The Shifter must have stolen the Indigo Star and turned the dragon against us. There's no other explanation."

The crowd murmured and nodded in agreement.

Samlett stood. "I'm afraid our friend Hockmar is right. We have to assume that the Shifter now has the Indigo Star, which means we're in for a war! Not only do we have to fight the Shifter, but we'll have to deal with the dragon Naytin, as well. We must organize our forces immediately, I say immediately."

Ari fumbled in the folds of her skirt. The Royal Scepter hung there, a reassuring weight. "Scepter?" she whispered. "What will happen now that the Star is gone?"

"The unicorns of the Celestial Valley will fade to shadows — shadows ruled by the Shifter. Already the blue band has lost its colors. Soon, the other bands of the rainbow will follow."

Ari's heart turned to ice. She closed her eyes for a moment. The din of the room receded. She had to be brave. She had to. "Will Naytin go back to sleep?"

"Eventually," came the cross little voice. "After the Star is restored to it, of course. It's Naytin's to guard. It always has been."

"And the colors will return to the blue band in the Celestial Valley," Ari murmured. Because this wasn't a question, the Scepter didn't reply.

"What do we do in the meantime?"

"You must search for the Star and give it back to the dragon."

The door to the back of the Inn banged open. Ari closed her hand over the unicorn head to keep it quiet. A cold breeze eddied into the room, making the fire in the hearth dance.

Two tall warriors stood just outside the Inn — two of the tallest people Ari had ever seen in her life. Both of them wore their wheat-colored hair in two long braids. Round metal shields protected their chests. Their arms were bare and strongly muscled. The woman wore a leather skirt that just topped thigh-high leather boots. The man had on leather breeches that reached his ankles. His feet were bare.

In the dimness of the night behind them, Ari could make out two unicorns. They were of the Warrior class, with thick legs, short powerful necks, and bold eyes. They had no jewels at the base of their horns.

The two humans ducked their heads to get through the door and moved slowly into the room. Behind them followed three more tall warriors. They were all dressed in leather vests and pants and tall boots that came up to their knees. They carried long spears that looked like javelins. The villagers murmured and fell silent.

"Who are they?" asked Lori.

Finn's mouth hung open, and a look of awe washed over his face. "I've . . . I've never seen them before," he whispered, barely moving his lips. "But I've heard tales."

"Who? Who?" Lori demanded.

The warriors made their way through the crowded room to the head table. The tall man in front said to Samlett, "You are host of this Inn? May I speak?"

Samlett nodded and sat down.

The warrior stepped around the table to face the audience. "My name is Armis." His voice boomed out over the room. "And my mates and I are Dragonslayers!"

This announcement caused quite a stir among the Resistance. Some gasped. Others whistled. A few people cheered.

One man stood and bellowed, "Nonsense! There are no Dragonslayers in the world anymore. Haven't all the dragons disappeared?"

"Not all of them. Most have gone away, but our people live on," said Armis. "Although we are now forest-dwellers and live off what the wilderness provides, we have kept the traditional ways alive all these years. We know how to capture and kill a dragon."

"This news is a blessing," said a woman, standing at her table. "If these people are truly Dragonslayers and they can defeat the dragon Naytin, then we will be free to fight the Shifter!"

"Here! Here!" shouted the others, clapping their hands and stamping their feet. "There's hope yet for the Resistance to win back the throne and free the Royal Family!"

Ari didn't know what to think. They were here to kill the dragon? Ari watched the woman Dragonslayer step around the table.

"My name is Valona," the Dragonslayer said. "Our plan is to follow the dragon back to Blue

Mountain." Valona's voice was level and sure. "We hope to attack the dragon there before it can fly again."

"But why do you want to attack the dragon?" Ari asked. Everyone stared at her. Ari stood up. "I mean, Naytin is gone now, gone back to Blue Mountain, where it belongs. What is the point in killing it?"

"The point is that it will come again," said Valona, her tones clear and crisp. "The dragon has left its lair because someone has stolen the Indigo Star. Therefore, the dragon is interested in only two things: eating from the lake, and destroying everything in its path until it finds the Star or until the Star is returned."

"Then why not return the Indigo Star to Naytin?" Ari asked.

"Who is that girl?" someone said from the middle of the room.

"Why is she arguing with the Dragonslayers?" asked another. "Can't she see that they want to help us?"

Armis responded, "The girl is being true to her heart, and she has asked a good question—a question that deserves answering. The truth of the matter, young lady, is that we are Dragonslayers, not thieves. We know not how to steal the Indigo Star from the Shifter, and to be honest, I'm not sure that anyone can accomplish that. What we *do* know is how to slay a dragon."

"Here! Here!" the people shouted.

Ari sat down. She felt a bit frustrated and embarrassed. It didn't seem right to her, killing the dragon for something that wasn't its fault. The dragon had been wronged, after all.

Besides, there *was* someone who could steal the Star back from the Shifter — the same person who had stolen the Royal Scepter. Ari could do it. She *had* to do it.

"We have come here to ask for volunteers," Valona said. "There are only five of us Dragonslayers left, although centuries ago we numbered in the hundreds. We have some small children, but none of them are dragon-slaying age. If five others will travel with us, to help us carry our tools and equipment and set up and break down camp, we will make better time and possibly stop the dragon before it can attack again. We will not ask these people to help us slay the dragon, only to cut a day or two off our journey."

The room suddenly went quiet. Although there were many people who wanted the dragon slain, there were, apparently, none who wanted to be involved in the actual slaying.

Ari stood up. She knew that the Dragonslayers would have to pass by Castle Entia to reach Blue Mountain. If she could travel with them as far as the Shifter's castle, then steal the Indigo Star, she could return the Star to Naytin and save the dragon's life.

And the lives of the unicorns of the Celestial Valley.

"I volunteer!" Ari declared.

"What?" said Samlett.

"W-w-what?" Runetta stammered.

"Are you crazy?" Lori nearly shouted.

Finn stood up, too. "And I volunteer," he said. Ari smiled.

"Oh, I can't believe this," said Lori. "I just can't believe it. The whole world is nuts." Lori looked over at Finn and then stood up. "All right, I guess I volunteer, too."

"That's three," said Ari. "And my dog, Lincoln, and my unicorn will come along, too. That makes five. Do you accept our offer?"

"Wait!" said Samlett. "You can't —"

"We accept," said Valona. "I like your courage, young miss. You will do a fine job, I'm sure."

Armis nodded. "I agree. It's settled, then. We leave at dawn!"

"Dawn?" remarked Lori. "Can't a girl get *any* sleep in this ridiculous world?"

10

❦

"**M**ilady, *please*, I beg you not to go." Samlett looked pitiful when he begged. His lips turned up and his eyebrows peaked.

Ari shook her head. It was early. The sun had barely risen over the forest surrounding the village. "I'm sorry, Samlett. It's the only way."

They all stood outside what remained of the stable behind the Inn: Ari, Lori, Finn, Lincoln, Chase, Tobiano, Samlett, and Runetta. Although it was only dawn, the whole town was out and about. There was so much work to do — rebuilding homes and barns — and life didn't stop for these people just because their houses were destroyed. There were crops and animals to tend, clothes to mend, and the market must go on.

The Dragonslayers had packed their wagons the night before, and they were ready to go. They were the finest wagons Ari had ever seen, with tall, sturdy wheels and axles made of iron. Their unicorns were hard-nosed Workers with broad chests and necks as thick around as tree trunks.

"Samlett," said Ari. "We both know that this is the best thing for me to do. First of all, the last place in the world the Shifter and his spies will look for the Princess of Balinor is with a group of Dragonslayers going out to kill a dragon."

"Second," Finn chimed in, "we're headed right for the Castle Entia, and if we're going to win this war against the Shifter, we've got to get that Indigo Star back. This is our best chance."

Runetta shook her head. "Oh, I know it looks like the best thing to do, but it's so dangerous. If you fail . . . if you fail —"

"There will be no talk of failure," Toby said. "I wish that I were going with you. I'd run my horn clean through the Shifter's evil heart."

Valona and Armis approached. "We're ready," Valona said. "It's normally a two-day ride to Sixton. We hope to cut that in half by riding hard all day, traveling through the night, and sleeping in shifts. The sooner we get started, the better."

"Oh, great," Lori said. "This sounds like it's going to be a marvelous trip."

Finn couldn't have been more excited. "Let's go!" he said, jogging over to the wagon and hopping up on the back of it.

Lori frowned. "You can sometimes be very annoying."

Finn winked at her. Lori blushed. Ari sighed deeply.

They said good-bye and hugged Samlett, Runetta, and Toby. Valona put her strong arm over Ari's shoulder and led her to the wagons. "It was brave of you to volunteer," she said.

"It was crazy," said Lori.

Valona and Armis explained their plan. It was simple and direct. They'd travel from Balinor to Sixton in a fast march. Then they would sail overnight on the *Dawnwalker* across the Sixth Sea to Demonview. The trip across Demonview to Blue Mountain was long, Armis explained; they hoped to cut it down by simply making better time. The faster they got to Blue Mountain, the better.

And then they'd have a dragon to slay.

Ari had other plans. When they came within sight of Castle Entia, she would abandon the Dragonslayers, sneak into the Shifter's lair, and steal the Indigo Star. She would carry the Royal Scepter. It could still answer questions, even if its magic was blocked, and if she asked the right questions, she'd have a good chance of slipping unnoticed in and out of the Shifter's castle. Then she and Chase would race to Blue Mountain ahead of the Dragonslayers to give Naytin the Indigo Star, save the dragon's life . . .

And restore life and color to the blue band of the unicorns of the Celestial Valley.

Things weren't getting any easier. Ari didn't

78

want to think about the risk involved in her plan. If Ari failed, what would become of Atalanta and the Celestial herd? And what about Balinor? What would happen to her people? Would her parents and brothers be safe? And what about Lincoln, Lori, and Finn — was it fair of Ari to bring them on this journey? What kind of dangers would they have to face because of her?

You can't think that way, said Chase.

Ari looked up to see the Sunchaser trotting beside the wagon. She reached out and patted his neck.

Together, he said, *we can do anything. Together we can conquer the Shifter. We will be victorious, milady, or die in the attempt!*

Ari patted his neck. "I will not die just yet, Chase! And neither will you!"

11

At Castle Entia, the servants cowered in the corners and whispered in the halls.

The master was in a rage. Since he had returned from Blue Mountain with the fabulous jewel, he had neither slept nor eaten. The head cook was so terrified he was going to be punished, he hid in the tunnels beneath the castle. The serving maids were too afraid to go into Entia's tower — and too afraid to stay away.

And in the tower, Entia cursed the Princess and her Bonded unicorn.

All the magic in the universe, and he couldn't use it.

The Shifter prowled the cold stone floor in his tower. He had shifted into a panther. The cruel claws and razor-sharp teeth suited his mood. He shook his sleek head and growled. His eyes glowed lion-yellow. He switched his long black tail and prowled around and around the pedestal that held the Indigo Star.

The great jewel lay in a pool of its own light. The six points of the stone pulsed with magic.

Magic the Shifter couldn't use. Not with Naytin on the hunt. The power of the stone was so great, the dragon would know instantly where it was. And Naytin would destroy Castle Entia as he . had destroyed the Village of Balinor.

Entia curled his panther lips in a mirthless grin. Word of the devastation in Balinor had reached him quickly. Everything had gone according to plan. He couldn't take the chance of using the Indigo Star magic just yet.

Not while that monster flew the skies! The heart of the Shifter's kingdom, the source of his evil magic, lay within Castle Entia. And if Naytin could destroy a village — one castle would disappear in an instant under his dragon breath.

It was night. His spies had been out. The Dragonslayers and that cursed Princess were on their way to Blue Mountain. Good. Very good. The Shifter wanted no one to interfere with Armis and his quest.

The sooner Naytin was dead, the better.

Entia shifted into human form. Black hair flowed down his shoulders and a black beard fell almost to his waist. He shrugged a dull gray cloak around his shoulders and pulled the cowl over his head.

He gazed on the Indigo Star and brooded. Could he chance using the magic against the dragon, its former master? He stroked his beard with long-nailed fingers. He preferred the human form. Normally, humans were weak and small and ungraceful, but with the magic of the Star he could be a giant — as strong or stronger than any unicorn he had ever known and more graceful than a swan.

But more than anything else, the Shifter favored human hands and fingers. He loved the way they held and touched and felt things. He loved the way the Indigo Star felt in his grasp, the feel of its power, its heat, its magical energy. Nothing in the world compared to human fingers and hands. He reached out to the magic jewel, his mouth open, panting slightly.

He drew back. Control — he must maintain control. He couldn't use the magic. Not until Naytin was slain. Unless . . .

Unless he had the Royal Scepter. The two combined, Star and Scepter, would mean that he could conquer all.

Entia spun in a sudden move and faced the door to his tower. The Shifter felt Kylie's presence slithering toward him. Her evil was pure — the Shifter admired that — but her power was nothing compared to his own. He allowed her to snake her way into his tower before saying, "Good evening, Kylie. What do you want?"

The Shifter felt a tremor of fear escape Kylie's snakelike heart.

"Masssster," she said. "Forgive me for intruding. I did not mean to disssssturb you."

"I'm sure you didn't, Kylie. In fact, I'm sure you were hoping to find me asleep or gone from my room. Isn't that right?"

She backed away, perhaps fearing the Shifter's wrath. "Oh, no, masssster. Of courssssse not. I only meant to —"

The Shifter's human hand shot out faster than the eye could see and snatched her by the neck. She gasped and choked in his powerful grip. The length of her coiled body twisted helplessly. "What were you looking for, Kylie? Tell me the truth. I can see into your heart. If you lie to me, I will know it."

"I heard the rumor, masssster, that you sssstole the Indigo Sssstar from the great dragon Naytin, and I only wanted to gazzzze upon it. I only wanted to ssssee what it looked like." She eyed the glowing sapphire hungrily. "I sssswear thissss issss the truth. I sssswear!"

The Shifter laughed. "You sound frightened, Kylie. You *should* be afraid. I am now the most powerful creature in the world. Don't ever think that you can sneak up on me again. You're lucky that I can still use you." He levitated off the floor and crossed his legs, floating in midair. His eyes were malevolent pools of red. "I have a job for you. I need to ensure total victory. I need the Royal Scepter. With the Scepter back in my possession, no one will ever stop me from ruling the world. That fool Sunchaser and the Princess are on their way to Blue Mountain with the Dragonslayers. I want you to follow them. And, in the middle of the fight with the dragon, you are to get the Scepter back for me. Do you think you can handle that task, Kylie?"

"Yessss, yessss, massssster, I can do it. I promisssse I won't let you down."

The Shifter settled gently on the floor. Kylie backed away and curled fearfully into the corner of the room. "Of course you won't fail me, because if you do . . . well . . . if you do . . ." The Shifter purposely left his sentence unfinished. He knew that Kylie's own imagination would come up with something far worse than he could say.

His laughter followed her as she slithered out the door.

12

ightmares troubled Ari's sleep on the first day of the journey with the Dragonslayers. The road had been rough, and the noise of the wagons and the unicorns and the Dragonslayers' equipment rattling and clanking had kept her awake for hours. When they reached the *Dawnwalker* Ari was exhausted. She lay down in a cabin and slept away the entire crossing of the Sixth Sea.

Lincoln's cold nose woke her when they reached the shores of Demonview. "Good grief," said Lori when Ari stumbled sleepily on deck. "And I thought *I* was a good sleeper. You haven't been conscious for hours."

Their feet no sooner touched shore, and they were off again, Dragonslayers, unicorns, wagons, Ari, Lincoln, Chase, Lori, and Finn. They camped in the evening, and Ari helped unpack and feed the unicorns and pitch the tents. She ate with the others and slept again.

Ari finally felt a little stronger when she woke up the next morning. Lori and Finn were feeling better, too. Lincoln, being a dog, had slept fine on the wagon and didn't look tired at all. And the unicorns seemed tireless. They weren't at all like the horses on the other side of the Gap, where Ari had stayed for a time at Glacier River Farm, where Atalanta had sent her to hide from the Shifter. Unicorns could ride for a long time without rest, with very little food and water, and nothing seemed to bother them. On the other hand, horses needed to rest and eat and drink all the time, and they were bothered by things like insects and cows — and even loud noises.

As far as Ari could tell, they were only a half-day's journey from Castle Entia. The Dragonslayers would not be traveling through the Valley of Fear and the Fiery Field. They would go straight through the Forest of Ardit to Blue Mountain. Very soon Ari would have to leave her companions behind.

She raised an eyebrow at Chase. Obediently, he slowed his steps. They waited until the rest of the group was slightly ahead of them.

"We should leave now, Chase."

"We can't just slip away, milady. Armis and Valona will come looking for us. We will have to tell them what we're up to. And they will want to know how we think that the two of us can battle the Shifter and rescue the Indigo Star."

Ari walked forward without speaking. The forest was growing dark and thick. Hardly any light shone through the trees. It was getting more difficult to set a quick pace through the dense trees and tangled vines. "I do have a plan," she admitted, "but it depends . . ."

Chase froze, his muscles rigid. His ears pricked forward. He stood protectively in front of her. "Watch out, milady," he said quietly.

Then, suddenly, they were surrounded by a band of shabbily dressed men and women. Ari jumped, startled by their sudden appearance. She raised one eyebrow. Somehow, they all looked familiar. The men and women carried clubs made of wood and knives of stone. The clothes they wore were tattered and old.

"Stop right there," said one of the men. "What are you doing in Demonview?"

Armis drew his unicorn to a halt, then turned and rode back toward them. It was Armis who spoke. "We're just passing through, friend. We don't want any trouble. We're Dragonslayers on the way to Blue Mountain."

"Dragonslayers? There haven't been any Dragonslayers around for a hundred years or more."

Armis's teeth gleamed white. "Although our numbers have dwindled, there have always been Dragonslayers."

The men and women looked threatening. Ari's heart began to beat faster. She couldn't allow anyone to stop her now. "The great dragon Naytin is awake. You know this, living here in the forest." Ari stepped forward. "Just two days ago, the dragon destroyed Balinor Village and it's likely to strike again and keep destroying things unless somebody does something about it."

A short, powerfully built man stared at her. His clothes were torn and tattered. He was as filthy as a barn animal. But his eyes seemed to shine unusually bright in the darkness. He was clearly the leader of these refugees.

"It's *you!*" he said at last. "I remember you." He turned to the others in his band. "Friends, she's the girl who freed us from the Pit. Look, it's her, I'd know her anywhere!"

The others came closer, gathering around. "It's true!" said one of the women. She dropped her club, walked up to Ari, and hugged her. The others came, too. "Thank you, thank you so much," they said, holding her, touching her. "You set us free. You released us from the Pit."

"What's all this about?" Valona said.

"Oh, it's just the slaves of the Shifter who were stuck in the Pit," Lori said. "Ari and I let them out of their chains when we got the Royal Scepter back from you-know-who. They must have escaped to these mountains. Gee, you would think they'd want to thank me. I was there, too."

Valona looked puzzled and a little angry. "Royal Scepter? What's this about the Royal Scepter?

We heard that it was lost the day of the Great Betrayal, when Entia abducted the King and Queen of Balinor. What would the likes of Ari be doing with it?"

"It's a long story," said Lincoln. "We'll tell you all about it later."

"I'm so glad that you're still free," Ari said to the men and women. She was touched by their gratefulness.

"Alas, not all of us are free," said the man. "Many of us were recaptured by the Shifter's shadow unicorns and forced back into service."

"Oh, no. I'm so sorry," Ari said. "Why are you still here in the forest? Why didn't you run away?"

"We couldn't. Many of our friends, our husbands and wives and sisters and brothers are still enslaved. We've made a pact — all of us have — to fight against the Shifter's forces until all our loved ones are free."

"You are brave men and women indeed!" said Armis, clapping his hands together.

"Friends," said Ari. "Maybe you could do *me* a favor now."

"Anything!" the man said. "Anything at all. We are at your service."

"I need to get into Castle Entia. I have unfinished business with the Shifter. If you can help me, you'll do a great service to your cause as well as mine."

"What are you talking about?" asked Valona.

"We're all on our way to Blue Mountain to challenge the dragon."

"No," said Ari. "You're on your way to Blue Mountain. I can't go the rest of the way with you because I've got a responsibility of my own to take care of, and I'm afraid I can't even tell you what it's about. You'll have to trust me. I know it's a lot to ask, but —"

Armis shook his head and folded his arms across his chest. He gave Ari a forbidding stare. "But nothing. This is out of the question. I'll not let you wander off with strangers — no offense to these fine people — in the Shifter's woods."

"She'll be in good hands," said the slave leader, who didn't appear to be offended at all. "We would all die before we'd let any harm come to the person who freed us."

"No, I won't hear of it," Armis insisted. "If Ari has to go to the Shifter's castle, then we'll all go with her. Together."

Ari didn't know what to say. Finn stepped forward. "It's all right, Armis. We must let her go. Whatever Ari has to do now, she has to do alone. The more of us who go with her, the more difficult it will be for her to succeed. All I can tell you . . . all I can say . . . is that Ari's mission is of grave importance in the war against the Shifter. The success or failure of the Resistance rides upon her shoulders."

Finn's words brought tears to Ari's eyes. She wanted to walk up to him and hug him tightly. But instead she mirrored the smile he had on his face. And felt her cheeks turn red.

She only needed enough supplies for two days: food for Lincoln and Chase, who, she decided, would wait outside the Castle while she stole inside, her father's knife, and the Royal Scepter. It didn't take her long at all to pack these things. She gave Lori and Finn a quick hug, and bade farewell to Armis and Valona. She fit Chase's saddlebags over his hindquarters, and slipped off into the forest with the freed slaves. She was surprised at how much fun they were to travel with, talking and laughing and sometimes even singing.

She never would have believed that people who had lived through such difficult times could be so cheerful. Ari could learn a lot from these good people. They had gone through hard times, but they didn't give up on life. Their troubles only seemed to make them stronger.

Ari turned to the leader, Luke, and said, "I'm not looking forward to walking through the Valley of Fear or the Fiery Field again."

"Well, guess what?" said Luke. "You don't have to worry about that at all."

"I don't? Why not?"

"Because we used to live and work every day in the Shifter's Pit. We know where all the underground caverns and tunnels lead. We can take you underground safely all the way to the rear entrance of Castle Entia."

Ari was grateful for this stroke of luck. It would be a way for her, Chase, and Lincoln to hide from the Shifter and his shadow unicorns. "Could you really? I would be forever grateful."

"Ha! Listen to the girl," said one of the women in Luke's band. "*She* would be grateful to *us*." They all laughed and traveled onward.

Just outside the Valley of Fear, Luke uncovered a secret entrance, and one by one they crawled down into a huge underground cavern. "Follow me!" said Luke. He lit a huge torch and started marching.

Ari dismounted Chase, walked behind Luke, and held the Royal Scepter tightly in her hands. The Scepter seemed to give her courage.

Ari concentrated on the journey. The underground world of Luke and his freed slaves was truly amazing. They had guard posts set up along the way, where people had to know secret passwords to pass through. Men and women carried food, water, and clothing back and forth. There was even a small medical station set up, where people with injuries could go to get treatment.

There were so many twists and turns in the trail that Ari had no idea where they were. She only knew where they were going — straight to the back door of Castle Entia!

Finally, when Ari's legs were so tired she didn't think she could take another step, Luke held up his hand for everyone to stop.

"Around that next bend," he said to Ari, "is a short tunnel that runs up to the surface. You'll be just outside the Shifter's rear gate. In another few hours, the slaves will enter the castle to serve the Shifter's dinner. When that time comes, we can slip you in as a servant. After that, you're on your own. None of us can help you with the Shifter. Whatever your business is with that foul creature . . . well . . . I hope you know what you're doing."

Luke's voice was kind and concerned. Ari nodded. She didn't really know what she was doing. But she had the Royal Scepter. She had the element of surprise. And she knew what had to be done. She must get the Indigo Star! Without it, the dragon would be slain. Without it, the Resistance was doomed to fall under the evil magic of the Shifter.

Worst of all, the Celestial Valley would fall into shadow. Forever. Atalanta's beautiful violet coat would be forever without light. The rainbow itself would fade to perpetual shadow.

"You might as well take a nap," Luke said. "Get some sleep before you go in there. We've traveled a long way today. You'll need all the rest you can get."

Luke showed Ari a well of water for Chase. She unpacked a package of oats, and set out some bean cakes for Linc. She and the collie and the unicorn didn't speak much. The time for words was past. She brushed Chase's mane, then combed burrs out of Lincoln's coat. Without a word, the great

93

unicorn and the dog went to a corner of the huge tunnel and settled into sleep. Ari curled beside them and took the Royal Scepter out, sheltering it from view with her arms. She stroked the beautifully carved rosewood head.

"How do I take the Star from the Shifter? I don't even know where to find it or what to do once I'm inside the castle."

The wooden head blinked in the torchlight. "The Shifter never sleeps. He wears the Star around his neck. Except when it rests on a pedestal in his tower."

"Where is the Star now? Can you tell? Or must I search for it?"

The Scepter seemed to be concentrating. "I can feel it moving," the unicorn head said finally. "Being this close to the Indigo Star — it's changing me, Your Royal Highness. I am different." The head swiveled on the rosewood shaft and gazed at her. The indigo eyes blazed with excitement. "I no longer have to wait for a question! All magic has an affinity, you know. Being this close to this great source of power — I feel it! There is magic in me, Princess, that you must learn how to release!"

Ari shook the Scepter a little to get its attention. "First we have to get the Star. If it's moving, does that mean the Shifter is wearing it?"

"Yes," the Scepter said.

"How will I steal the Indigo Star from him if he never sleeps and it's around his neck?!"

94

"Don't *panic*, Princess," the carved head said crossly. "Do you remember about the three levels of magic?"

"Of course!" Ari whispered.

"Then tell me again!"

Obediently, Ari recited, in the quietest voice she could manage:

"Three levels of magic: The first magic is small.
The kind that is done without effort at all.
First magic can turn sweet milk to sour
Or cure stomach upsets or help crops to flower.

The second is mighty and fierce, you will find;
The second belongs to the Dreamspeaker's kind,
And the Shifter, as well, for it helps him disguise
His terrible form from most human eyes.

The third type of magic is deep, not controlled
By humans or those in the unicorns' fold.
Third magic made both the Shifter's dark hand
And Atalanta the Good and her unicorn band.

It begins at the end. It ends at the start.
I guard its gate. The Old Mare is its Heart."

Then for the very first time she could remember, the Scepter asked Ari a question. "Now you tell me — what kind of magic will defeat the Shifter?"

95

"The strongest magic, of course — the magic that made you and the good unicorns. The Old Mare is its heart!"

The Scepter made a derisive noise like *phuut!* and said loftily, "Don't be too eager to show the Shifter your power. He is very powerful, too, and he will sense my magic in the same way that I am affected by the nearness of the Star. He wants me more than anything in the world — it's what he's searching for now, and he'll stop at nothing to get me back."

"Then what do I do?" asked Ari. "How do I defeat the Shifter without the strongest magic?"

"Sometimes it is the thorn that defeats the lion, Princess. 'The first magic is small, the kind that is done without effort at all.' "

"I'm not sure I understand," Ari said.

But the Scepter was silent. Ari shook it lightly, but it refused to answer any more questions. Finally, she curled protectively around the Scepter and fell fast asleep.

And Ari dreamed.

She dreamed of the Celestial Valley and its vibrant colors. She dreamed of the deep blue river and the mysterious Watching Pool. She dreamed of the Celestial unicorns in all the brilliant colors of the rainbow. Atalanta was there, in all her violet-and-silver glory. Then the Dreamspeaker faded into nothingness. In the distance, Ari could see the other unicorns. Some of them were as pale as ghosts!

Ari's lips moved, and she cried, "Atalanta!"

The Dreamspeaker whispered, *"Time is running out. The Indigo Star must be returned to the dragon soon. Remember, Princess Arianna. The Shifter never sleeps! The Shifter never sleeps!"*

"Atalanta!" Ari cried. She jerked awake. She was sweating.

"No, it's just me, Luke." Luke smiled down at her. Ari came fully awake and sat up sharply.

"That must have been some powerful dream you were having," said Luke. He handed Ari a cup of water and some fresh bread. "I thought I'd better wake you up. Go on, have a bite to eat and drink. In a few moments the servants will be near the rear gate of Castle Entia."

"Thank you," said Ari. She ate the bread quickly and washed it down with the water.

Sometimes it is the thorn that defeats the lion, the Scepter had told her. *The Shifter never sleeps,* Atalanta had said. *The Shifter never sleeps.*

What did it all mean?

She sat back against the cave wall, closed her eyes, and waited.

13

Ari woke to the touch of Luke's hand on her shoulder. She blinked in the dimness, confused for a moment. Where was she?

She looked up into Luke's kind, concerned face. Oh, yes! She was in the tunnel, waiting to go to the castle. Waiting to meet the Shifter. She swallowed hard, then smiled at Luke. "I must have fallen asleep again!"

"My friends from the castle are here, Ari. Are you ready?"

"I'm ready!" Then, to herself, "As ready as I'll ever be!"

She followed Luke to the mouth of the tunnel. Luke crawled out the hidden entrance. A cluster of people stood among the trees and shrubs guarding the tunnel. They were dressed in drab browns and grays, the uniform of the castle's servants. Luke signaled to the woman who was in the lead. He spoke to her for only a few moments, then returned to Ari with a large hooded cloak in his hands.

"Put this on," he said. "All the servants wear these, and you'll be able to hide your staff inside it." He winked and smiled.

Ari wondered if Luke had guessed her true identity. It didn't matter. Even if Luke suspected she was the Royal Princess, he would never say a word to anyone. She put on the cloak and tucked the Scepter inside it, hugging the rosewood staff close to her ribs.

"It's a good fit," said Luke. "I've arranged everything with the lead servant. Every evening, she is the one who sees to it that the Shifter's meal is prepared and served to his liking. When the time comes, she will tell you to deliver the Shifter's dinner to his private chamber in the tower. The rest is up to you."

"Thank you for all of your help," Ari said to Luke.

"And thank you for yours," Luke replied. "Together we will beat the Shifter. One day, all of my people will be free." He kissed her gently on the forehead.

Ari climbed out of the tunnel and fell in line behind the lead servant. They walked out of the darkness, onto the torch-lit path that led directly to the rear gate of Castle Entia.

None of the servants said a word as they walked past the two shadow unicorns guarding the rear gate. The shadow unicorns didn't even seem interested in their passing. "No one will defeat the master now that he has the Indigo Star," said one of the unicorns to the other. "Soon the Shifter will rule the world."

Ari set her jaw in determination. Not if she could help it!

Once inside, they walked down a long, narrow corridor into the kitchen where the lead servant began telling people what to do. Some were ordered to gather and cut fruits and vegetables. Others were told to bake the bread or chill the wine or prepare a hot tea. She told Ari to begin arranging the plates and silverware on a tray for the Shifter's dinner. "The master prefers to eat like a human being these days," she said, "using spoons and forks and knives with his hands."

Finally, the meal was ready. The servant woman told Ari to carry the Shifter's tray. Then she led Ari around a maze of hallways to the foot of a long, winding set of stairs.

"This is the stairway that leads up to the Shifter's tower. There is only one way up or down. I'm usually the person who brings the master his dinner, but I doubt he'll notice the difference."

"Thank you," said Ari, making sure the Royal Scepter was pressed firmly against her body.

The lead servant pulled back her hooded cloak, revealing a kind but weary face. "I've often thought that if I had the courage . . . if my heart was just a little stronger . . . maybe, just maybe . . . if I took a knife with me from the kitchen —"

Ari reached out and held the servant's hands. The woman's fingers trembled, and her skin felt cold and clammy. "No. You mustn't think that way. You're a good woman. There are other ways — better ways — to defeat him."

The woman nodded. "Yes. There are girls like you, with more courage than I will ever know."

Ari didn't know what to say to that. She didn't feel very courageous. In fact, if there was anywhere to run and hide, anywhere at all — no, no, she must go on. For her people. For her family. For the Celestial Valley.

Ari began the long walk up the steps to the Shifter's tower. She held the dinner tray in her hands and kept the Royal Scepter tucked between her arm and her body.

The stairway seemed to go on forever. Ari was out of breath by the time she reached the tower. She stood outside the Shifter's chamber for a moment and waited for her heart to stop pounding — only it didn't seem to want to slow down. Ari was afraid — more afraid than she'd ever been in her life.

She still didn't have any plan for when she walked through the Shifter's door. If the Indigo Star was around his neck, as the Scepter had told her, how would she get it without revealing her true identity? Wouldn't she need all of her powers to steal the Star from the Shifter?

Atalanta didn't seem to think so. And the Scepter had reminded her, *The first magic is small, the kind that is done without effort at all.*

Well, if she stood outside the Shifter's chamber all night, she wouldn't accomplish anything. She balanced the tray on one hand and knocked on the door.

The Shifter didn't answer, but the door slowly drew open.

Ari stepped inside. The room was hot and dark. It smelled sour, like something rotten. She felt the Shifter's presence, although she could not see him.

Ari suddenly realized that the servant woman hadn't told her where to place the Shifter's tray. She looked around for the most likely place and decided on the desk in the center of the room.

"The tray doesn't go there!" said the Shifter. "How many times do I have to tell you? Bring it here." A horrible chuckle escaped him. "Am I that repulsive?"

The sound of his voice sent chills up Ari's spine. She didn't want to get any closer to him. She was terrified. How would she ever steal the Indigo Star if she couldn't even force herself to look at him?

She carried the tray deeper into the chamber, where the Shifter was sitting. He looked almost human, except he was twice as large and muscular as any man that Ari had ever seen, including Armis. His skin had a slightly swampy look.

Around his neck, on a silken length of rope, hung the Indigo Star! It was absolutely brilliant, the most majestic jewel Ari had ever seen! She was only a few steps away from it now, but there might as well have been miles of ocean and desert standing between them.

"I'll ask you again," the Shifter said. "You are human. Look at me. Am I so repulsive to you?"

Ari tried to clear her mind. *The Shifter never sleeps*, Atalanta had told her. "No," Ari said, her voice nearly faltering. "You look tired. Aren't you getting any sleep?"

The Shifter looked surprised. "What's this? An honest answer?" He stood up and turned his back to Ari, gazing out the window of the tower. "The truth is, I have not been sleeping at all. I am so powerful that I no longer need to sleep."

"Yes, master. But maybe you would *like* to sleep. Sometimes it feels good just to close your eyes and rest."

He turned around again and looked at Ari. She felt her knees weaken, and her legs nearly gave out from under her.

"An interesting thought," the Shifter said. "Do you think sleep will make me look more human?" He held his hands out in front of him and studied them.

"Yes, I think so, master." Ari's voice trembled.

"Maybe I will try it, although I am not in the least bit tired." He went over to his bed and lay down. Then the Shifter closed his eyes. "Get out."

"Yes, master."

She walked over to the door and stepped out of the Shifter's chamber. But she did not close the door behind her. Instead, she reached inside her cloak and removed the Royal Scepter. She could feel the rosewood staff warm in her hand.

Sometimes it is the thorn that defeats the lion. The first level of magic would be so small, so trifling, that the Shifter wouldn't even notice it. He was far too powerful now to care at all about minor magic. He didn't think it could hurt him. All he could think about was power, power, and more POWER.

So Ari concentrated on the Shifter's eyes. She thought about how heavy they must feel, how tired they were from not resting, not sleeping. She didn't know very much about magic, but there was some part of her, maybe a part of her that was born to it, that knew just what to do.

Ari thought about how the Shifter must long to close his eyes, to sleep, even if it was only for a few minutes.

As she thought these things, the Royal Scepter became warmer in her hands, and she could feel the slightest bit of magical power reaching out of the Scepter, moving toward the Shifter's bed. The magic was no more noticeable than a drop of dew on a leaf, or the steam rising out of a teacup.

Sleep, whispered the magic. *Sleep. Sleep.*

Ari watched the magic curl around the Shifter's head. It was there and gone in a wink. The Shifter's coal-red eyes closed. His chest rose and fell in a rhythmical way.

And all was quiet.

Ari was afraid to move. If the Shifter awoke when she approached the bed, he would discover her. If he was asleep, she was afraid she might wake him.

But the Indigo Star! She *must* take it!

Ari stepped into the Shifter's chamber on the tips of her toes. Slowly, silently she made her way to the side of his bed.

She reached for the silken rope — and the Shifter made a sound!

Ari froze.

The Shifter's eyes remained closed. He made the sound again.

It was a snore — a soft snore. The Shifter was asleep! He was snoring!

Ari took the silken rope in her hand, but she was afraid to take the Star from around the Shifter's neck. She didn't want to chance even the slightest movement of his head. Instead, she carefully pulled the knot around, untied it, and slipped the Indigo Star free.

Ari immediately felt the power of the Star surge up her hand and into her body. It kicked the strength back into her legs and made her fear disappear.

The Shifter sat up straight in bed —

He saw Ari holding the Indigo Star —

He shrieked — a horrible, nightmarish howl!

The Shifter grabbed Ari's wrist.

"Push the magic!" the Scepter cried. "Let it go. Release it!"

Ari felt the power of the Star. It was a mighty river, and she was in its way, like a dam holding it back. She squeezed her eyes shut and PUSHED!

The Star lashed out like lightning!

The strike jolted the Shifter so hard it flung him out of bed and threw him against the far wall. He hit the floor like a giant load of bricks.

"RUN!" the Scepter commanded. "To the window!"

Ari raced to the window of the tower. She stepped onto the ledge. The ground was at least a hundred feet below her. Above her, the wide-open sky stretched out forever in the night.

"Join me with the Indigo Star!" the Scepter commanded. "Hold the Star above me!"

Ari held the blue jewel just over the unicorn head. It didn't seem possible that the radiance of the Star could grow any brighter.

But it did!

A glorious blue light wrapped the Star and

the Scepter together. Ari heard the Shifter shriek in fear. The blue light expanded in a tidal wave of brilliance. The light washed up Ari's arms and circled her head.

And in the light of this Deep Magic, Ari saw the Celestial Valley!

For a moment, she forgot that she was poised on the ledge of the Shifter's tower. She saw the deep green fields and the majestic blue of the Imperial River.

And she saw the Celestial unicorns!

Ari held her breath. She had never seen anything so beautiful. The rainbow herd was gathered under the Crystal Arch. Their heads were raised expectantly. At the very end of the rainbow stood a pale, white unicorn with a crystal horn. Her violet eyes looked deep into Ari's own. Then, as if a blue sun had risen and painted the Dreamspeaker with light, Atalanta's color returned. Her coat turned the color of twilight, deep purple shading to violet.

The violet-lavender-indigo light continued to spread. Behind the Dreamspeaker, the blue band of unicorns also sprang to vivid color.

"Arianna!" the Dreamspeaker called. "Walk the path! Walk!" Ari glanced down. The magic spread a blue bridge of light from the window ledge to the ground far below.

She walked on the air, on the path of magic, and reached the courtyard.

Above her, she heard the Shifter's shriek of

rage. And then, two familiar figures emerged from the thorny brush surrounding Castle Entia.

"Lincoln!" she cried. "Oh, Chase!" She raced to her unicorn and leaped on his back. She felt the familiar surge of power beneath her. "To Blue Mountain, Chase! We have a dragon to save!"

14

While Ari, Chase, and Lincoln raced over the countryside, Ari thought about the Indigo Star, and how the simplest magic of all allowed her to take it from the Shifter.

She thought about Atalanta, the Celestial Valley, and the Celestial unicorns. Their colors would be restored!

She thought about her parents and two brothers, and how they might soon be free if she could rally her loyal forces and defeat the Shifter.

So much was possible now that she had the Indigo Star and would return it to the great dragon Naytin, and to its rightful place in the mountains.

With so many things to think about, Ari wasn't surprised at all to see Blue Mountain suddenly coming into view. It was daybreak now, and a soft glow hung over the forest and the valleys below.

On the shores of Pearl Lake, the sight of the

monstrous dragon filled the landscape. Having just fed from the lake, its silvery hide glistening morning light, the remains of weeds and fish still hung from its gigantic jaws.

And there were the Dragonslayers, moving into position to wage an attack against the dragon. Ari could see their long javelins. She saw Armis and Valona and the other slayers. Lori, Rednal, and Finn stood beside the wagons.

Ari was just in time! She reined Chase and circled the dragon at a trot. Naytin seemed not to notice her at first, but Ari knew better. The beast's eyes and instincts were sharp. And the magic of the Indigo Star was strong. The dragon would sense it. Ari would have to be very careful.

"Naytin!" Ari shouted. "I have something that belongs to you." She kept Chase at a trot around the dragon so that it wouldn't be able to attack her.

"Give it back!" the dragon snarled. Ari could feel its horrible anger.

"I will give it back, but first you must hear the truth."

"The truth? I'll tell you the truth. You stole the Indigo Star!"

"*NO!*" said Ari. "It was the Shifter who stole the Star from you. I have taken the Star back from the Shifter to return it to you."

Naytin grunted. Its flat black eyes rolled at her. It was a considering look.

"You must promise not to attack me or my friends, and I will gladly give it back to you."

"Always tricks. You humans are full of tricks."

"No tricks. A simple promise." She urged Chase to a canter, then a hand gallop. She moved so fast that not even the dragon's eyes could follow.

"*WHY SHOULD I BELIEVE YOU?*" Naytin roared.

Ari had no choice but to act now. She saw that the Dragonslayers were getting closer, moving in to attack. She tapped Chase's side with her heels. She, Lincoln, and her unicorn pulled to a halt in front of the dragon. Ari dismounted and placed the Indigo Star down on the ground beside the lake and stepped quickly back from it. "There it is —" she said. "Your Star!"

Now was the most dangerous moment. She saw the Dragonslayers Armis and Valona come out of the woods near the lake. The other slayers were already behind the dragon, their sharp javelins winking in the morning sunlight.

Naytin growled, its tail lashing back and forth.

"It belongs to you," Ari said. "And I have brought it back."

The dragon bent down and snatched the Indigo Star off the ground.

"Ari!" Armis yelled to her. "Move quickly. You're in danger, and you're in our way."

111

"No," Ari answered. "You will *not* attack the dragon."

Naytin looked up and saw the slayers. "Dragonslayers!" it snarled. Its giant muscles tensed. Its black eyes were slits of rage. It was ready to attack.

"No, Naytin, we have a deal," Ari said. "I have returned your Star, and you promised not to attack me or my friends."

"But they are Dragonslayers."

"They will listen to me."

Ari turned to Armis and Valona. Lori and Finn came toward her. She took out the Royal Scepter and held it high above her head.

"You will not attack!" she cried. "I am Princess Arianna of Balinor!"

Armis and Valona looked at her for a moment, clearly shocked. They turned to the others — to Chase, Lincoln, Lori, and Finn — and said, "Is it true?"

They all nodded. Armis and Valona dropped to their knees, laid down their javelins, and bowed before her. "Your Royal Highness," said Valona. "We are at your service."

Ari turned back to the dragon. "We have a deal. I'm not here to harm you, only to return what's rightfully yours. Do you believe me now?"

Naytin gripped the jewel in its claws, almost as if the dragon couldn't believe it. "You are true to your word, Princess. You honor your people and your kind. I will attack you and your kind no more."

With that, the great dragon stretched out its massive wings, lifted itself gently into the air, and flew back to its lair. In a few moments, the dragon disappeared inside the mountain, back to its resting place, with the Indigo Star safely returned to where it belonged.

The Deep Magic was gone! Ari felt it drain from her, like water from a pool. She collapsed on the shore of Pearl Lake. The others ran to her.

"Princess! Princess!" They all gathered around and helped her sit up. She drank a cool flask of water and ate some bread.

"Thank you," she said when she finished.

"How did you do it?" barked Lincoln, wagging his tail happily. "How did you get the Indigo Star?"

Ari hugged Lincoln and scratched behind his ears. "It's a long story," she said.

"I can't wait to hear it!" Finn said.

"I'm sure it's boring," sighed Lori.

"We all want to hear what happened to Ari — I mean the Royal Princess," Armis's strong voice boomed out.

"And we also want to know where and why you've been away from the throne of Balinor for so long," said Valona firmly. "And how the Dragonslayers can help you regain your throne."

Ari stood up. She was so happy she could hardly hold back her tears. "I will tell you everything, I promise," she said. "But I will tell the tale as we return home." She looked up and scanned the skies. "The Indigo Star is back where it belongs," she said quietly. "And soon, the Shifter will have recovered from his fear and be on the hunt for us." She leaped to Chase's back and raised her hand. "Let's ride!"

They all gathered behind her. The Sunchaser trotted gracefully down the shore of Pearl Lake. Sunshine glistened brightly along the water.

And then, suddenly, as the sunlight crept fully over the mountain range, the great bronze unicorn leaped into a gallop. The wind blew back his mane and a fine mist from the lake sprinkled Ari's face.

Chase rode hard and fast, and as Ari sat upon Chase's back, for a moment, there was only the bond with her unicorn to fill her heart with joy. There was only sunlight and wind and the feel of the earth moving beneath them at incredible speed. There was no Shifter, no evil in the world, no throne to recapture.

There was only unicorn and rider, at peace and at play, as there had been since the beginning of time.

But how long would it last?

About the Author

Mary Stanton loves adventure. She has lived in Japan, Hawaii, and all over the United States. She has held many different jobs, including singing in a nightclub, working for an advertising agency, and writing for a TV cartoon series. Mary lives on a farm in upstate New York with some of the horses who inspire her to write adventure stories like the UNICORNS OF BALINOR.

Meet the Guardians of the Force.

STAR WARS®

JEDI APPRENTICE

- ☐ BDN51922-0 **#1: The Rising Force**
- ☐ BDN51925-5 **#2: The Dark Rival**
- ☐ BDN51933-6 **#3: The Hidden Past**
- ☐ BDN51934-4 **#4: The Mark of the Crown**

Scholastic Inc., P.O. Box 7502, Jefferson City, MO 65102

Please send me the books I have checked above. I am enclosing $_____ (please add $2.00 to cover shipping and handling). Send check or money order–no cash or C.O.D.s please.

Name_____Birthdate_____

Address_____

City_____State/Zip_____

Please allow four to six weeks for delivery. Offer good in U.S.A. only. Sorry, mail orders are not available to residents of Canada. Prices subject to change.

SWA599